STORIES OF THE CHRISTIAN HYMNS
Revised Edition

Helen Salem Rizk

Abingdon Press

STORIES OF THE CHRISTIAN HYMNS

Fourth Printing 1993

Copyright ©1964 by Carroll E. Whittemore
Revised edition copyright ©1986 by Abingdon Press
All rights reserved.

ISBN 0-687-18300-6
Printed in the United States of America

FOREWORD

No one really knows how many hymns have been written in the history of the Christian church. Some authorities say over three million; some say over five million; and some say more. Isaac Watts alone wrote over two hundred in less than two years; sixty-five hundred are attributed to Charles Wesley the "sweet bird of Methodism"; and Fanny Crosby, the blind hymn-poetess, completed at least eight thousand singable hymns.

STORIES OF THE CHRISTIAN HYMNS is a basic collection of sacred songs and the unusual events which inspired their writing. There is a drama in the story of the hymns—a drama of courageous struggle, earnest conviction, consecrated dedication, and spiritual victory. This modest volume tries to capture this drama and to present it briefly, accurately and in an interesting manner to aid the reader to a wider understanding of our cherished hymns, to assist in attaining a greater knowledge of the old favorites, and to be one more voice in preserving the beauty, dignity, and power of Christian hymns for future generations.

By necessity this book has to be limited; but an attempt has been made to include the favorites of everyone. We hope yours is here. And we hope you will be encouraged to love and to sing the old-time hymns which have been the power and strength of generations of Christians through the ages.

A CHARGE TO KEEP I HAVE
Charles Wesley, 1707–1788

ı eighteenth-century hymn by Charles Wesley. Sung to the tune of "Old Kentucky" by remiah Ingalls, this revival hymn could be heard swelling from tent and camp ground over America. About a hundred years after it was written, Lowell Mason composed the ısic which is used presently.

A charge to keep I have, A God to glorify,
A never-dying soul to save, And fit it for the sky.

A MIGHTY FORTRESS IS OUR GOD
Martin Luther, 1483 –1546

ırtin Luther, one of the outstanding figures in the history of the Protestant Church, in no eater way served his fellow Christians than in the writing and composing of one of the ɔrld's best loved hymns, "A Mighty Fortress Is Our God." It was written in the late ımmer of 1529. The famed German theologian, after a long period of deep depression, ɪd found spiritual comfort in the strength of Psalm 46. He repeated over and over the ɔrds, "God is our refuge and strength, a very present help in trouble." With this thought mind, he hurled his defiance at all his foes, physical and spiritual, the struggles of mind ıd body, the opposition of pope and people, and penned these words never to be rgotten by mortal men:

A mighty fortress is our God,
A bulwark never failing;
Our helper He, amid the flood,
Of mortal ills prevailing.
For still our ancient foe,
Doth seek to work us woe;
His craft and power are great,
And armed with cruel and hate.
On earth is not his equal.

ABIDE WITH ME
Henry Francis Lyte, 1793 –1847

his famous hymn, written September 4, 1847, by Henry Francis Lyte, almost was not ritten at all. Life had not been easy for him, and at the age of fifty-four, this famed nglish clergyman, serving as vicar of Lower Brixham in Devonshire, was advised by his octor to save his health by wintering in Italy. He was determined to administer Holy ommunion once more to his congregation. And on the first Sunday of September in 847 he did exactly that, even though the ravages of tuberculosis left him weak and xhausted. After the service he strolled by the sea until sunset thinking of the abiding resence of God and working on a hymn poem started many years before in the early ays of his ministry. He was really too tired to complete the poem and thought of putting aside until his return from Italy. However, some inner compulsion pressed him to finish le last line. That evening he placed the completed line "Abide with Me" in the hands of is family. He never returned from Italy, dying two months later on November 20. If he ad waited until he returned, one of the world's most famous hymns would not have been ritten.

ALAS! AND DID MY SAVIOR BLEED

Isaac Watts, 1674 –1748

Written by Isaac Watts one of the greatest hymn writers of all time (he wrote over six hundred hymns), "Alas! and Did My Savior Bleed" appeared in a volume of poems published in 1705 entitled "Hymns and Spiritual Songs." A very unusual man, Watts served as minister of the English Congregational Church, preaching his first sermon when twenty-four years of age. History says that though he was a charming man, his stature was small and his physical appearance hard to believe. Only five feet in height, his face was sallow with a hooked nose, small beady eyes and deathlike pallor. One lady, a Miss Elizabet Singer, who had fallen in love with his poetry and thought she had met her soul-mate at la refused his hand in marriage when she finally saw him, with the remark, "I admired the jew but not the casket!" However, his hymns have been jewels admired by all generations of Christians.

ALL CREATURES OF OUR GOD AND KING

St. Francis of Assisi, 1182–1226

In July 1225, one of the great Christians of all times, St. Francis, ill, blind, and lonely, came to a little group of buildings called St. Damian just outside the village of Assisi in Italy. Depressed and tired he found peace in this quiet little refuge with the sounds of birds and animals, which he always loved, and the kind care of a group of women called the Poor Clares. It was here, just one year before his death, St. Francis wrote a simple, beautiful hymn which has stood the test of ages. It praised the wonder of God's creation and reflects St. Francis' love of the simple things of life:

> All creatures of our God and King,
> Lift up your voice and with us sing
> Alleluia, alleluia!
> Thou burning sun with golden beam,
> Thou silver moon, with softer gleam;
> Thou rushing wind that art so strong,
> Ye clouds that sail in heaven along,
> O praise Him, alleluia!

ALL GLORY, LAUD, AND HONOR

Theodulph of Orleans, Ninth Century

"All Glory, Laud, and Honor" written by Theodulph Bishop of Orleans in the ninth century, one time freed its author from death in the dungeon. The story is told that on Palm Sunda 821, King Louis the Pious, son of Charlemagne, while celebrating the day with his people, glimpsed the radiant face of Theodulph through the bars of the prison where he had been confined. The king had experienced trouble with his relatives and had suspected Theodulph of supporting them. Thus he had cast him into the dungeon. Now as he passed by, he saw the brave saint and heard his voice singing with joy "All Glory, Laud, and Honor," a song h had written himself. The king was so pleased at the evidence of religious devotion that he released Theodulph at once and restored him to his ecclesiastical position.

ALL HAIL THE POWER OF JESUS' NAME

Edward Perronet, 1726–1792

Edward Perronet, born in 1726 in the quaint village of Shoreham, was the son of a minister who served as vicar of this village. A giant cross stood facing the hill whe

Vincent Perronet enjoyed a long and holy ministry. Young Perronet received profound inner inspiration not only from his father, but also from John Wesley who frequently visited their parish. Perronet and Wesley remained friends, even though they differed in the question of lay administration of the Sacraments. Eventually he became a minister of an independent church in Canterbury. It was in 1779 while serving as vicar at the Canterbury Cathedral that "All Hail the Power of Jesus' Name" was written. The majesty of the words:

> "And Crown Him,
> Crown Him, Crown Him
> Crown Him Lord of all"

has reflected the power and glory of Christ to Christians the world over.

ALL THE WAY MY SAVIOR LEADS ME
Fanny J. Crosby, 1820 –1915

There is no end to the unusual stories told about Fanny J. Crosby, the blind poetess author of this hymn and scores of other gospel songs. "All the Way My Savior Leads Me" is the outcome of one of those dramatic moments. One day in 1874, Miss Crosby, who was short of money and with no time to reach her publishers for advance payments, simply knelt and prayed for five dollars, which was her immediate need. She had hardly finished her prayer when the doorbell rang. Upon opening the door she was greeted by an admirer of her hymn tunes. According to Miss Crosby, when the stranger left he shook her hand and pressed five dollars into it. From this experience she wrote:

> All the way my Savior leads me,
> What have I to ask beside?

ALL THINGS BRIGHT AND BEAUTIFUL
Cecil F. Alexander, 1818 –1895

A hymn for children written in 1848 by C. Frances Alexander and taken from her volume called "Hymns for Little Children." Sung to the tune of an old English melody, this hymn emphasizes the eternal truth that God is the author of all beauty, all wisdom, and all creation. Each little flower that opens, each little bird that sings, each purple mountain, running river and ripe fruit in the garden, all are products of his everlasting majesty.

ALMOST PERSUADED
Philip Paul Bliss, 1838 –1876

Gospel hymn written by Philip Bliss in 1870 while waiting for a train in Ohio. The famed gospel hymn writer had slipped into an Ohio church one Sunday night a few moments before his train was scheduled to leave. While here he heard the minister read from the book of Acts: "Then Agrippa said unto Paul, almost thou persuaded me to be a Christian." Bliss recognized immediately a good theme for a hymn, and thus one of the outstanding gospel hymns was born.

AMAZING GRACE
John Newton, 1725 –1807

John Newton wrote "Amazing Grace" in 1779; and only he could write this hymn with such meaning. "Amazing Grace" was the story of his life. Every word was pulled with pain from the dark days and the treacherous times of his early sea-faring youth to the wondrous joy of his discovery of the love of God. His epitaph, written by his own hand, tells more eloquently than any other words the extent of depth and height he experienced: "John Newton, clerk, once an infidel and libertine, was by the rich mercy of our Lord and Savior, Jesus Christ, preserved, restored, pardoned and appointed to preach the faith he had long labored to destroy." Every line of his hymn is filled with tears of remorse because of the greatness of his sin, and expressions of joy because of the discovery of God's grace:

> Amazing grace, how sweet the sound,
> That saved a wretch like me;
> I once was lost but now am found,
> Was blind but now I see.

AMERICA THE BEAUTIFUL
Katherine Lee Bates, 1859 –1929

Katherine Lee Bates, author of "America the Beautiful," daughter of a clergyman, was born in Falmouth, Massachusetts, in 1859. After graduating from Wellesley College she became a full professor of English literature of that college in 1891. While on her way to Colorado Springs to teach in a summer school, she stopped in Chicago during the Columbian Exposition in 1893. The tremendous beauty of the Colorado fruited plains and the "alabaster city" of the World's Fair became the inspiration for writing this hymn. These words have been sung in every corner of the world substituting "Australia" for "America," or when sung in Canada, the refrain reads, "O Canada, O Canada"; even in Africa the missionaries sing, "O Africa, O Africa." But all nations can join and sing together:

> God shed his grace on thee,
> And crown thy good with brotherhood,
> From sea to shining sea.

ANGELS, FROM THE REALMS OF GLORY
James Montgomery, 1771–1854

This Christmas hymn is one of James Montgomery's favorite compositions. Montgomery, one of the greatest of the Moravian hymn writers, wrote the hymn in 1816 and it is considered one of the most challenging hymns ever written. The tune going under the name "Regent Square" was written by Henry Smart a blind composer of London, England. His physical vision may have been impared, but Smart could see as few men are able to see. From the combined vision of these two men has come one of the immortal Christmas classics.

> Angels, from the realms of glory,
> Wing your flight o'er all the earth;
> Ye who sang creation's story,
> Now proclaim Messiah's birth:
> Come and worship, Come and worship,
> Worship Christ, the new-born King!

ART THOU WEARY, HEAVY-LADEN
John Mason Neale, 1818 –1866

This ancient Latin hymn, translated into English by John Mason Neale in 1862, was President Franklin D. Roosevelt's favorite hymn. The original text can be traced back a r as John of Damascus whose nephew Stephen, in the eighth century A.D., then hoirmaster of the community of monks in the famous Marsaba Monastery of the Eastern hurch in the Kidron Valley of Palestine, composed this hymn which proved to be his masterpiece. The eloquence and influence of this song of the church is attested by the ct that it has lived over a thousand years after its author's death.

> Art thou weary, heavy-laden;
> Art thou sore distressed?
> "Come to me," He saith, "and coming
> Be at rest!"

AWAY IN A MANGER
author unknown

his quiet little Chistmas song is often called "Luther's Cradle Hymn" and is considered y many authorities to have been written by him sometime during the early sixteenth entury. More recently it is thought to be of German Lutheran origin in early Pennsylvania. o matter who the author may have been, this lovely carol lullaby is sung over and over gain to children of every land and language during the Christmas season. It is one of eir first encouragements to learn and to love "the little Lord Jesus."

BENEATH THE CROSS OF JESUS
Elizabeth Cecilia Clephane, 1830–1869

his hymn of Christian experience so popular as a solo for the male voice was written by woman. Elizabeth Cecilia Clephane was about thirty-five years old when she wrote the ymn near Scott's Abbotsford Abbey in England in 1865. Four years later she was dead. lthough she lived only thirty-nine years, most people could live to be a hundred and not ccomplished half what she did in the writing of two of the world's beloved hymns: Beneath the Cross of Jesus" and "There Were Ninety and Nine."

BE STILL MY SOUL
Katharina von Schlegel, 1697–1765

atharina von Schlegel, born in Germany in 1697, was the author of this hymn of Christian xperience. Very little is known of its origin or of its author except that it was discovered and anslated by Jane L. Borthwick (1813–1897). It is thought that Katharina von Schlegel was ead of a Woman's House of the Evangelical Lutheran Church at Gothen, Germany. No oubt one of the reasons for the great popularity of this hymn is its music. It is set to the mous melody of Sibelius, "Finlandia," one of the most stirring and beautiful melodies ever ritten.

BEULAH LAND
Edgar Page Stites, 1836–1916

"I've reached the land of corn and wine,
And all its riches freely mine."

his old gospel hymn written by E. P. Stites was first sung at Ocean Grove, New Jersey, a great conference of Methodists. It became an immediate favorite the world over and as sung not only by Methodists but by congregations of every denomination since the ne of its origin. Ira Sankey, the famed song leader who teamed up with Dwight L.

Moody to make one of the most famous evangelistic duos of American church history, speaks of this hymn as being one of the most requested at funerals.

Blessed Assurance, Jesus Is Mine
Fanny J. Crosby, 1820 –1915

Fanny Crosby's contribution to the Christian world through music is enhanced by another favorite, "Blessed Assurance, Jesus Is Mine," a song of true salvation. Her personal faith in Christ shines like a light in every verse. The stirring tune to this hymn which arouses many congregations to sing with great power and emotion was written by Phoebe P. Knapp.

Blest Be the Tie That Binds
John Fawcett, 1740 –1817

The drama of this famous hymn centers around a loving congregation, a woman who spoke her mind, and a Baptist minister who refused a call to one of the largest churches in England. In the summer of 1772, the Rev. John Fawcett, whose family had "increased faster than our income," was overjoyed with the receiving of a "call" to the famous Carter's Lane Baptist Church in London. Immediately, preparations were made to transfer to this greater opportunity. A great loyalty and devotion had developed between pastor and people, and although they gave their time and strength willingly to help him pack, they did not hide their reluctance about letting him go. When the final day of moving came, the wagons arrived early and loading of boxes and bundles began. Finally only one box remained, in the middle of the dining room. Rev. Fawcett noted that his wife stood near it in deep thought. "What's the matter?" he asked. Her reply was slow and thoughtful, "Do you think we are doing the right thing?" she asked. "Where will we find a congregation with more love and help than this?" The minister was silent a moment, then he replied, "I think you are right, dear. I have acted too hastily. I was so overjoyed to think that I would have a better home and a larger salary for you and the children that I did not really pray about it." Together they walked to the porch and explained to their people that they had decided to remain.

Break Thou the Bread of Life
Mary A. Lathbury, 1841–1913

Mary A. Lathbury, talented artist and writer, became associated with the famous "Chautauqua Movement" in 1877, when she was hired as an assistant to Dr. John H. Vincent, secretary of the Methodist Sunday School Union. She spent the summer of her thirty-fifth year at the assembly grounds on the quiet shores of beautiful Lake Chautauqua in the Finger Lakes region of western New York. One day as she and Dr. Vincent were standing by the lake watching the sunset, the Methodist bishop asked her if she would write a hymn to be used by the Chautauqua Literary and Scientific Circle. Miss Lathbury agreed and began to think of a possible theme. As she meditated about the blessing that had been received at the summer conference she related the thought to the multitude that had been fed with bread on the hillside by Galilee. Thus came to life the words which Christians have come to know and to love.

Breathe On Me, Breath of God
Edwin Hatch, 1835 –1889

The beauty of Edwin Hatch's hymn poem "Breathe on Me, Breath of God" was not discovered until after his death in 1889. His early years had been spent in Canada, first as professor of classics in Trinity College, Toronto, and then as Rector of the High School, Quebec. Even though later at Oxford, England, he received fame as church historian an

heologian, it was while he was among the peaceful lakes and beautiful rivers of eastern
Canada that he was moved to write this little gem of prayer to God.

CHRIST THE LORD IS RISEN TODAY
Charles Wesley, 1707–1788

"Christ the Lord Is Risen Today" a resurrection hymn written by Charles Wesley, one of the
famed Methodist Wesley brothers, appeared first in 1739 in a volume called "Hymns and
Sacred Poems." Wesley's inspiration for this hymn came from a fourteenth century Latin
composition "Jesus Christ Is Risen Today." It was first called "Hymn for Easter," and has
known wide popularity from the time it was written. Of all of Wesley's hymns this one is
sung the most:

> *Christ the Lord is risen today, Alleluia!*
> *Sons of men and angels say, Alleluia!*
> *Raise your joys and triumphs high, Alleluia!*
> *Sing, ye heavens, and earth reply, Alleluia!*

COME, WE WHO LOVE THE LORD
Isaac Watts, 1674 –1748

Isaac Watts probably wrote more hymns than any other person who has ever lived. "Come,
We Who Love the Lord," written in 1709, is no doubt, the only hymn that he or anyone else
wrote, which was used to end the threatened strike of an unhappy choir. It is told that a New
England church was experiencing a difference of opinion within the congregation. The
argument had progressed to such an extent that the choir had become rebellious. Dr.
Samuel West, the pastor, received word that the choir was going to express its displeasure
by refusing to sing on the following Sunday. The minister averted any trouble, cleverly and
uniquely, by announcing as the opening hymn "Come, We Who Love the Lord." After
reading the first verse through very slowly, he turned to the choir and requested that they
lead in the singing of the second verse:
"Let those refuse to sing
    Who never knew our God."
It goes without saying, that the choir could do nothing but abide by their pastor's resourceful
request!

COME, YE THANKFUL PEOPLE, COME
Henry Alford, 1810 –1871

Of all the harvest hymns, "Come, Ye Thankful People, Come," written by the Reverend Henry
Alford, dean of Canterbury Cathedral, is the most popular. It was first published in his Psalms
and Hymns in 1844. To describe Alford as precocious as a child is an understatement. He
started writing at the age of six, and by eleven had compiled a collection of hymns. At
sixteen these were his words: "I do this day as in the presence of God and my own soul
renew my covenant wth God, and solemnly determine henceforth to become His, and do His
work as far as in me lies." "Come, Ye Thankful People, Come" may not have been his most
scholarly effort, but it will always remain the most popular writing of his career.

DEAR LORD AND FATHER OF MANKIND
John Greenleaf Whittier, 1807–1892

Only a poet of John Greenleaf Whittier's depth and understanding could so successfully
challenge the world to forget for a while the stress and strain, the hurry and hustle, of

everyday life and responsibility and find in the quietness of meditation, a renewal of strength and faith of God. His hymn "Dear Lord and Father of Mankind" is one of the strongest voices leading people to the truth that in the still silence of their inner mind is found the beauty of God's loving care.

> *Dear Lord and Father of mankind,*
> *Forgive our feverish ways;*
> *Reclothe us in our rightful mind;*
> *In purer lives thy service find,*
> *In deeper reverence praise.*

ETERNAL FATHER, STRONG TO SAVE
William Whiting, 1825 –1878

This hymn is the national hymn of the Navy and is used at the United States Naval Academy in Annapolis and on English ships. In addition a beautiful French translation is a standard part of the hymn book of the French Navy.

FAIREST LORD JESUS
author unknown

This famous hymn had its origin in Germany in the seventeenth century, and was discovered in America in 1850 by Richard Storrs Willis, a musician and newspaperman, who wrote books on church music and other musical subjects. The tune is an ancient Silesian folk song derived from legend and story, which is a ballad picturing common life with its interests and enthusiasm. It was said to have been sung by the German Knight Crusaders on their way to Jerusalem in the twelfth century and is still referred to as the Crusaders' hymn, although no proof of this has been established. This hymn telling of the beauty of nature is often called "The Marching song of the out-of-doors" and is a favorite of young people. It is also interesting to note that pianist Franz Liszt used this tune in his oratorio "St. Elizabeth."

FAITH OF OUR FATHERS
Frederick William Faber, 1814–1863

There is no Christian hymn that lifts the soul or stirs the imagination more than "Faith of Our Fathers" written in approximately 1850, by Frederick W. Faber, Anglican clergyman of England. Yet the strange fact is that very few people realize the reason for his writing the hymn. Record shows that all his hymns were written after he was received into the Roman Catholic Church in 1846. One of Faber's views was that the true Church of England was continued through the Roman Catholic Church. This is what he meant when he spoke of the "faith of our fathers." However, this was a case of what he had written far exceeding the boundaries of what he had intended; and thus, Protestants sang the hymn with equal meaning and fervor as Catholics. It proves, once again, that the mass singing of hymns is one of the strongest expressions of faith in Christendom.

FOR THE BEAUTY OF THE EARTH
Folliott Sanford Pierpoint, 1835–1917

Folliott Sanford Pierpoint was twenty-nine years old when he sat on the green hillside late in the spring of 1864 outside his native city of Bath, England. The violets and primroses were in full bloom and the world was a beautiful place to see. As he sat down to rest and meditate he could not help feeling the wonder and glory of God around him. His glad

gers had wings of joy as he wrote word after word, inspired by the spreading springtime
auty:

> For the beauty of the earth,
> For the glory of the skies,
> For the love which from our birth
> Over and around us lies;
> Lord of all, to Thee we raise
> This our hymn of grateful praise.

GLORIOUS THINGS OF THEE ARE SPOKEN

John Newton, 1725 –1807

his joyous hymn is considered to be the greatest ever to come from the pen of the
everend John Newton, close friend of William Cowper. It was part of a collection by
ewton and Cowper called "Olney Hymns" which included two hundred and eighty of
ewton's and sixty-eight of Cowper's, and was in use in England at about the time of the
merican Revolution. Newton also wrote "How Sweet the Name of Jesus Sounds."

GOD BE WITH YOU TILL WE MEET AGAIN

Jeremiah Eames Rankin, 1828 –1904

n emotional hymn of prayer written in 1882 by Jeremiah Eames Rankin, a Congregational
inister of New England. His purpose for writing the hymn was to find a way for the
hristian to say good-bye which was not contradictory to his faith and belief. He finally
ttled for the phrase "God be with you," which he felt was the Christian way of saying
good-bye until we meet again." The story is told that Rankin invited two composers to write
usic for the words. One composer was well known, the other unknown. He chose the work
the unknown composer, William G. Tomer. He certainly must have been inspired in his
oice for there is no finer example of the harmony of words and music than in this hymn.
'ithout doubt, the popularity of "God Be with You Till We Meet Again" has been augmented
onsiderably because of the melody.

GOD OF GRACE AND GOD OF GLORY

Harry Emerson Fosdick, 1878 –1970

> God of grace and God of glory,
> On Thy people pour Thy power;
> Crown Thine ancient Church's story;
> Bring her bud to glorious flower.

his hymn was written by the Reverend Harry Emerson Fosdick for the opening services of
e new Riverside Church in New York City, October 5, 1930. It first appeared in a published
ymnal, *Praise and Service* in 1932. Two different hymn tunes are frequently used: a Welch
ymn melody by John Hughes, 1873–1932, and Regent Square, a tune by Henry Smart,
867, first sung in the Regent Square Presbyterian Church of London, England.

GUIDE ME O THOU GREAT JEHOVAH

William Williams, 1717 –1791

1785 Selina, Countess of Huntingdon, founded a college in South Wales to train "godly
nd pious young men" for the Christian ministry. Tradition says that she was not only a

beautiful woman, but one who had a sense of the dramatic. She acquired the "sweet singer" of Wales to celebrate the opening of the college with a new, original hymn. William Williams, as he was called, sang and played for the first time his own hymn poem "Guide Me O Thou Great Jehovah." Not only did it inspire the potential men of the cloth in great fashion, but it became a favorite hymn of generations to follow.

> Guide me, O Thou great Jehovah,
>   Pilgrim through this barren land;
> I am weak, but Thou are mighty,
>   Hold me with Thy powerful hand;
> Bread of heaven, Feed me till I want no more;
> Bread of heaven, Feed me till I want no more.

ȞARK! THE HERALD ANGELS SING
Charles Wesley, 1707–1788

Charles Wesley of England is without doubt one of the two most productive hymn writers of all time—the other being Isaac Watts. Yet, strangely enough, Wesley was able to get only one hymn poem into the Church of England's Book of Common Prayer—and that one by error! An eighteenth-century printer didn't know that the "established Church" of England frowned with disapproval on Wesley's hymns. He needed to fill an empty space in the Book of Common Prayer and took it upon himself to insert a Christian poem called "Hark, How All the Welkin Rings!" by an Anglican clergyman names Charles Wesley. When the error was discovered attempts were made to have it removed, but it proved so popular that it was allowed to remain. This is not the end of the story. "Hark! the Herald Angels Sing" still mighty not have reached its tremendous Christmas popularity if it hadn't been for other twists of fate. Wesley had called his poem "Hymn for Christmas Day" and it was sung with mild enthusiasm for over a hundred years. It might have slipped gradually into the mist of oblivion if it had not been for a tenor, William Haymen Cummings. When vocalizing on a bit of Felix Mendelssohn's "The Festgesang," he noticed how the arrangement was perfect for Wesley's "Hymn for Christmas Day." Retitled "Hark! the Herald Angels Sing" and strengthened by the powerful music of Mendelssohn, Wesley's hymn became one of the greatest Nativity songs ever composed. Written in 1738, one of the first of Wesley's hymns became one of his greatest.

ȞAVE THINE OWN WAY
Adelaide A. Pollard, 1862 –1934

"Have Thine Own Way" was written in 1902; the music, composed by George Cole Stebbins, was not written until five years later. Although Miss Pollard wrote many hymns and poems, "Have Thine Own Way" was the only one to survive the tests of time. However, this alone would justify her claim to fame; for this hymn became a favorite throughout all the Christian world.

ȞE LEADETH ME O BLESSED THOUGHT
Joseph Henry Gilmore, 1834 –1918

In March 1862, during the Civil War, twenty-eight-year-old Reverend Joseph H. Gilmore, son of a New Hampshire governor, was supplying in a historic old Philadelphia church, the First Baptist Church at Broad and Arch Streets. Because of the dark depression of the war between the states, Gilmore selected as a theme the Twenty-Third Psalm, emphasizing

God's leadership during dark days. Over and over again he repeated the phrase, "He leadeth Me." Later at the home of one of the deacons, Gilmore was so filled with the thought of his theme that he was unable to contain himself. Seizing a piece of paper, he jotted down these lines: "He leadeth me! O blessed thought; O words with heavenly comfort fraught." When he finished there were four stanzas and a chorus. Gilmore promptly forgot all about what he had written; but his wife, recognizing something good, sent a copy to a Boston periodical. It was here that William Bradbury, famous composer and publisher of church music, discovered it and set it to music.

His EYE IS ON THE SPARROW
Mrs. C. D. Martin, 1867–1948

This beautiful gospel hymn was written because of the courage and faith of a woman bedridden for more than twenty years. Mrs. C. D. Martin and her husband were visiting Mr. and Mrs. Doolittle of Elmira, New York. Both of the Doolittles were "incurable cripples," but in spite of their handicaps carried on their business in a courageous manner. Greatly impressed by the faith of the saintly couple Dr. Martin commented upon the spirit and joy of his host and wife. Mrs. Doolittle's reaction was simple and direct, "His eye is on the sparrow and I know he watches me," she said. Mrs. Martin, who wrote many hymns and poems immediately recognized the potentiality of the phrase, and before the day ended she had arranged and incorporated it into one of the most touching hymns of all time.

Holy, HOLY, HOLY! LORD GOD ALMIGHTY
Reginald Heber, 1783–1826

One of the greatest hymns of all ages, "Holy, Holy, Holy" was written in 1826 by Bishop Reginald Heber. It was based on the meter of the Apocalypse as found in Revelation 4:8-11: "Holy, Holy, Holy, Lord God Almighty, which was, and is, and is to come." The famed English poet-bishop wrote the hymn especially for Trinity Sunday as a tribute to the Trinity. It is one of the few hymns written for a specific Sunday of the church year, yet equally adaptable for every other Sunday. It is said of this hymn that it is found in more hymn books than any other hymn written.

Holy SPIRIT, TRUTH DIVINE
Samuel Longfellow, 1819 –1892

The Reverend Samuel Longfellow shared the distinguished talent of poet with his famous brother Henry W. Longfellow. An ardent theist and devoted pastor, he spent his life in active service to others. Ill health was the reason for his early retirement from the ministry, as well as his desire to write the life of his beloved brother. Earnest devotional emotion is evidenced in his hymn "Holy Spirit, Truth Divine," which was published in 1864. Deep mysticism pervades in every stanza of this great hymn and opens the channels toward God for our prayers.

How FIRM A FOUNDATION
author unknown

One of the truly great hymns of the church which has the unusual distinction of being absolutely anonymous. Most of the experts of hymnody agree that this hymn was written in 1787, most of them agree that it is one of the outstanding hymns of Christendom, but most of them also agree that the author is unknown. This hymn joins the long line of Christian activity which remain anonymous, but whose blessings are shared by the whole church.

𝕳OW GREAT THOU ART
authorship doubtful

Strangely enough, this truly impressive contemporary hymn received its present popular form through two different countries and two different translations. The original form was a Swedish poem "O Mighty God" by Carl Boberg written in 1886 and translated by Professor E. Gustav Johnson, of North Park College in 1925. The poem, based on the everlasting wonders and eternal powers of God had a metrical pattern that was easily identified with an old Swedish folk song and soon the words became a permanent part of that song. Before his death, Boberg had the joy of knowing his poem had become a cherished contribution to Swedish music. "O Mighty God" spread beyond Sweden and its native tongue. Soon it was popular in other countries, and sung in Russian, Polish, German, and other tongues. In 1923, the Reverend Stuart K. Hine, London missionary to the Ukraine, heard the song for the first time in Russia. Unaware of the fact that the song had originated in Sweden, Hine attributed it to a Russian prisoner and credited him with writing it in 1921. He was so impressed with the song that he made an English translation in 1948 which he called, "How Great Thou Art." The interesting fact of the story of this great hymn is that although two translations were made through three different languages, over thirty years apart, the might and grandeur of the hymn is preserved. "How Great Thou Art" inspires the human heart to the wonder and majesty of God.

𝕴 AM THINE, O LORD
Fanny J. Crosby, 1820 –1915

This gospel hymn written by Fanny Crosby has been a favorite of Christian Endeavor societies the world over. It was written on an occasion of the famed blind poetess' visit to Cincinnati, Ohio, at the home of W. H. Doane who has composed scores of popular gospel songs. They were sitting together in the still hush of the evening twilight hour talking about the nearness of God. The close fellowship of these two great Christians so impressed Miss Crosby that before retiring she had written the complete hymn. The next morning Mr. Doane fitted the music to the words and thus was born a special favorite of gospel hymn lovers wherever gospel hymns are sung.

> *I am Thine, O Lord, I have heard Thy voice,*
> *And it told thy love to me;*
> *But I long to rise in the arms of faith,*
> *And be closer drawn to Thee.*

𝕴 HEARD THE BELLS ON CHRISTMAS DAY
Henry Wadsworth Longfellow, 1807–1882

This lovely Christmas carol, written at the turn of the nineteenth century, was one of the few hymns authored by the eminent poet, Henry Wadsworth Longfellow. The phrase "Peace on earth, good-will to men" was the inspiration for this poem. The famed New England poet truly believed that God was powerful and strong enough to overcome the strife on earth and had vision far beyond his time of the day when all nations would live together in peace.

> And in despair I bowed my head;
> There is no peace on earth, I said,
> For hate is strong, and mocks the song
> Of peace on earth, good will to men.

Its ringing tune was written by John Baptiste Calkin. "Waltham" is also used as hymn tune in Doane's popular missionary hymn, "Fling Out the Banner."

𝕴 LOVE THY KINGDOM LORD

Timothy Dwight, 1752–1817

Timothy Dwight, D. D., president of Yale College, wrote "I Love Thy Kingdom, Lord" just after the American Revolutionary War. Critics of early American hymnody say that the use of Watts' "Psalms and Hymns" did not become general throughout New England because of the reference to English characteristics. Something had to be added and changed to make it palatable to the newly liberated American patriots. Timothy Dwight was the one to do it, with alterations to Isaac Watts' hymnal and new versifications. "I Love Thy Kingdom, Lord" was part of the new arrangement.

> I love Thy kingdom, Lord,
> The house of Thine abode,
> The Church our blest Redeemer saved
> With His own precious blood.

𝕴 LOVE TO TELL THE STORY

Katherine Hankey, 1834 –1911

Katherine Hankey was thirty-two years old when she wrote the hymn "I Love to Tell the Story." It arose out of a deep desire in her heart to tell the simple gospel story wherever she was in life. First, it was in the Sunday school of Clapham, England, where she became a devoted, refined consecrated woman. Then, it was in the heart of Africa, where she spent most of her life, giving the sales of all her writings to missions. Finally, it was in the hospitals of London, where she spent the last minutes of her life telling lonely patients of God's beautiful love. When Katherine Hankey wrote "I Love to Tell the Story" in 1866, she was doing more than expressng a feeling in her own being, she was projecting that same feeling into the minds of thousands of people through the years who would sing her song and receive the same challenge.

> I love to tell the story Of unseen things above,
> Of Jesus and His glory, Of Jesus and His love,
> I love to tell the story, Because I know 'tis true
> It satisfies my longings, As nothing else can do.

𝕴 NEED THEE EVERY HOUR

Annie Sherwood Hawks, 1835 –1918

Annie Sherwood Hawks, a thirty-seven-year-old Brooklyn, New York, housewife, wrote the words to this gospel hymn one morning in 1872 while she was doing her housework. On the following Sunday she showed her simple poem to the pastor of her church, the Reverend Robert Lowry, minister at the Hanson Place Baptist Church, who himself was a composer as well as a preacher. Lowry took them home, set them to music, added a chorus of his own, and a famous hymn was born.

> I need Thee every hour, Most gracious Lord;
> No tender voice like thine Can peace afford.
> I need Thee, O I need Thee,
>   Every hour I need Thee;
> O bless me now, my Savior, I come to Thee.

𝕴 WOULD BE TRUE, FOR THERE ARE THOSE WHO TRUST ME
Howard A. Walter, 1883 –1918

In July, 1906, Howard A. Walter, a Congregational minister, was teaching English at Waseda University in Japan. He sent his mother a poem he had written called "My Creed." In the poem he expressed the feeling that motivated him as a Christian:
"I would be true,
   for there are those who trust me."
His mother was so impressed with the sincerity of the poem that she submitted it to the editors of Harper's Bazaar, who published it in 1907. Three years later it was seen by Joseph Peek who saw its possibility as a hymn. Although a tune was running clearly in his mind, Peek was unfamiliar with the techniques of musical composition and got an organist friend to write it down while he whistled. "I Would Be True," one of the outstanding youth songs of all time, is one of the few hymns that mention the word "laughter" as a Christian attribute.

𝕴N CHRIST THERE IS NO EAST OF WEST
John Oxenham, 1852–1941

In 1908, Winston Churchill made the opening speech at a great missionary exhibition in London called "The Orient in London." Part of the exhibition was a pageant depicting the triumphs of the missionary cause. In charge of the pageant was a minister named Dugald Macfadyen, nephew of John Oxenham. Macfadyen persuaded his famous uncle to provide the music for the pageant; and part of the music was "In Christ There Is No East or West." This hymn which was so widely acclaimed in that day has never lost its significance; its plea for the fellowship of love has even more profound meaning in our world of today.

> In Christ there is no east or west,
> In him no south or north;
> But one great fellowship of love
> Throughout the whole wide earth.

𝕴N THE CROSS OF CHRIST I GLORY
Sir John Bowring, 1792–1872

The real inspiration of the hymn "In the Cross of Christ I Glory" came from the words of the apostle Paul, "God forbid that I should glory, save in the cross of our Lord Jesus Christ, by whom the world is crucified unto me, and I unto the world" (Galatians 6:14). The author, Sir John Bowring, published this hymn in 1825 and used only the first line of the scripture, altered a bit. Instead of emphasizing the experience of being crucified with

Christ, he brought forth the joy and cheer which fills the heart of the believer who realizes what is really meant by the redeeming work of Christ. On his gravestone are engraved the words of this his best known hymn:

> In the cross of Christ I glory,
> Towering o'er the wrecks of time;
> All the light of sacred story
> Gathers round its head sublime.

IN THE GARDEN
C. Austin Miles, 1868–1946

"In the Garden" is one of the favorite gospel hymns of all times. Its author and composer, C. Austin Miles, was born in 1868 in Lakehurst, New Jersey, and died in 1946, thirty-two years after the writing of this hymn. His musical career started at the age of twelve, at which time he played for his first funeral at the local Methodist church. In 1912 he was asked to write a hymn poem that would "breathe tenderness" and bring hope and rest for the weary. Miles visualizing Mary Magdalene at the Garden of the resurrection brought forth the words:

> And He walks with me, and He talks with me
> And He tells me I am His own,
> And the joy we share as we tarry there,
> None other has ever known.

IN THE HOUR OF TRIAL
James Montgomery, 1771–1854

James Montgomery born in 1771 in Ayrshire, Scotland, was the son of a Moravian minister and was educated in a Moravian school at Fulneck, near Leeds, England, for the Christian ministry. He spent more of his time writing poetry than studying. After leaving school in 1787 he spent four years in very precarious and doubtful modes of living, and was even twice imprisoned for his outspoken political opinions. He was classed by the literate as a minor English poet, but the church ranks him with Wesley, Watts, and Doddridge. From the four hundred hymns he wrote more than three hundred are widely sung today. Montgomery wrote "In the Hour of Trial" on October 13, 1834. He drifted away from the church and at the age of forty-three, like the prodigal son, returned to the old Moravian church of his boyhood, and later peacefully died in his sleep in 1854.

IT CAME UPON THE MIDNIGHT CLEAR
Edmund Hamilton Sears, 1810 –1876

A popular Christmas hymn written in 1850 by a Unitarian minister Edmund Hamilton Sears, born at Sandisfield, Massachusetts, April 6, 1810. Although most of his life was spent in the ministry (twenty-seven years at Wayland, Massachusetts), for twelve years he was associated with the Reverend Rufus Ellis in the editorial work of the *Monthly Religious Magazine.* It was here that most of Sears' poetical works were published.

> It came upon the midnight clear,
> That glorious song of old,
> From angels bending near the earth,
> To touch their harps of gold.

19

$\mathfrak{J}$T IS WELL WITH MY SOUL

Horatio Gates Spafford, 1828 –1888

Tragedy was associated with the writing of the words of this famous gospel hymn, and followed closely the composing of the music. H. G. Spafford wrote the poem on the mid-Atlantic over the exact spot where his four children had drowned a few days before. His wife and children were sailing to France on the *Ville du Havre,* one of the largest ships afloat. It was rammed by an English iron sailing vessel and sank to the bottom of the ocean within two hours, killing 226 people. Mrs. Spafford lived, but the four children were lost. Just weeks before this tragic drowning, Spafford had lost everything he owned in the great Chicago fire. And now, if not tested enough, he lost all of his beloved children. As soon as it could be arranged he sailed to Europe to join his wife. On the way, December 1873, the captain of his ship pointed out to him the spot where the tragedy had occurred. Here in the dark of night, with a heart heavy with grief and pain, but yet surging with faith and hope, Spafford wrote these words:

> *When peace like a river attendeth my way,*
> *When sorrow like sea-billows roll,*
> *Whatever my lot, Thou hast taught me to say,*
> *It is well, it is well with my soul!*

Philip Paul Bliss, great song leader and composer, wrote the music for this hymn in November, 1876. Two weeks after it had been written, Bliss and his wife were killed in a tragic train crash in Ashtabula, Ohio. It was said by witnesses that Bliss could have escaped, but chose to die by the side of his wife, who was caught in the flaming wreckage.

$\mathfrak{J}$ESUS CALLS US O'ER THE TUMULT

Cecil F. Alexander, 1818 –1895

This beautiful gospel hymn was written in 1852 by Mrs. Alexander. Based on Matthew 4:18-19 which contains the verse, "Follow me and I will make you fishers of men" this hymn is written in the simple, unadorned, emotional but refined style so typical of Mrs. Alexander. Used by some denominations as a hymn for St. Andrew's day "Jesus Calls Us O'er the Tumult" is a favorite in the hymnal of every church.

$\mathfrak{J}$ESUS, KEEP ME NEAR THE CROSS

William H. Doane, 1832–1915

In 1869, William H. Doane, famed composer of gospel music, wrote a hymn tune and handed it to the equally famed blind hymn writer Fanny J. Crosby with the request that she write words to fit it. She did promptly, and there came into being "Near the Cross," a gospel hymn popular in every decade since. A shadow of fate fell upon this hymn as it was being written. The words of the chorus said, "In the cross, in the cross, Be my glory ever, till my raptured soul shall find rest beyond the river." Strangely enough, forty-six years later both Doane and Crosby found their eternal rest—the same year.

$\mathfrak{J}$ESUS, LOVER OF MY SOUL

Charles Wesley, 1707–1788

The famed clergyman Henry Ward Beecher said of "Jesus, Lover of My Soul" that he had rather have written that hymn than have the fame of all the kings that ever sat upon the earth. Written by the master hymn writer, Charles Wesley in 1740, it was not considered by the author as one of his better hymns. In fact, it was not published until nine years after Wesley's death. However, the singing public has not agreed with Wesley's opinion and has made his hymn an all-time popular favorite. Many stories have circulated concerning the origin of the hymn. One tale tells of a flock of birds who flew in the window and found refuge under Wesley's coat. Other stories speak of savage storms at sea which prompted the author to pen his famous words. Still another source says that the hymn-poem resulted because of an angry mob which threatened Wesley's life forcing him to flee. The truth, however, is that the noted Methodist clergyman was simply praising God with one of the thousands of hymns which he left as a legacy to the world.

> *Jesus, lover of my soul,*
> *Let me to Thy bosom fly,*
> *While the nearer waters roll,*
> *While the tempest still is high.*

JESUS LOVES ME, THIS I KNOW
Anna Warner, 1827–1915

The hymn "Jesus Loves Me, This I Know," written in 1859, is an international favorite among children. It has been taught and sung in many tongues by missionaries the world over. The author, Anna Warner, wrote many hymns for her Bible class at West Point, and when she died a military funeral was held in her honor by the cadets whom she loved and taught for many years. The composer of this hymn, William Bradbury, developed the "Sunday-School song" form, which was a single ballad style verse with a refrain. It may be said that this was a true American contribution to hymnody.

JESUS, SAVIOR, PILOT ME
Edward Hopper, 1818 –1888

This seafaring hymn was written by the Reverend Edward Hopper who was born in 1818 and a graduate from Union Theological Seminary. His last pastorate was at the Church of Sea and Land in New York, a favorite place of worship for sailors and men of the sea. Although this song was composed for seamen and imitated the tossing of a boat by the ocean waves, its rhythm also accents the motion of a mother rocking her child. This gospel hymn found its place in hymnology as a hymn of spiritual trust. it first appeared as a poem in the *Sailor's Magazine* in 1871 and was published that same year in the *Baptist Praise Book.*

> *Jesus, Savior, pilot me*
> *Over life's tempestuous sea;*
> *Unknown waves around me roll,*
> *Hiding rocks and treach'rous shoal*
> *Chart and compass come from Thee,*
> *Jesus, Savior, pilot me.*

JESUS SHALL REIGN WHERE'ER THE SUN
Isaac Watts, 1674 –1748

The first hymn of significance written on the theme of world missions was in 1719 by Isaac Watts, "Jesus Shall Reign Where'er The Sun." Strangely enough this theme of

Jesus' kingship was taken from the Old Testament, Psalm 72: "He shall have dominion also from sea to sea. . . . They shall fear thee as long as the sun and moon endure . . . . All nations shall call him blessed. . . . Let the whole earth be filled with his glory."

> *Jesus shall reign where'er the sun*
> *Does His successive journeys run;*
> *His kingdom stretch from shore to shore,*
> *Till moons shall wax and wane no more.*

ℑESUS, THE VERY THOUGHT OF THEE
Bernard of Clairvaux, 1091–1153

David Livingstone, famed missionary of Africa, had these words to say about this fine old hymn of the Middle Ages. "The hymn of St. Bernard on the name of Christ pleases me so that it rings in my ears as I wander across the wide, wide wilderness." Dr. Livingstone believed, as many believed after him, that "Jesus, the Very Thought of Thee" was penned by the saintly Bernard of Clairvaux early in the twelfth century. However, most authorities conclude that it was written much later than that by an unknown author. Whatever the case, it is done with the same devout spirit and inspired style as used by the noted cleric of the Middle Ages. Translated in 1849 by Edward Caswall, "Jesus, the Very Thought of Thee" has long held a sacred place in the hearts of lovers of hymnody.

> *Jesus, the very thought of thee,*
> *With sweetness fills my breast;*
> *But sweeter far thy face to see,*
> *And in thy presence rest.*

ℑOYFUL, JOYFUL, WE ADORE THEE
Henry van Dyke, 1852–1933

The joyous music in this famous hymn is an arrangement from the famed composer Beethoven's *Ninth Symphony.* Many hymn writers had tried to create verse which would measure up to this which was some of the world's greatest music. It wasn't until a few years before the First World War, about 1911, that Dr. Henry van Dyke, while on a preaching visit to Williams College, finally succeeded in writing words that caught the fullness of the joy of Ludwig von Beethoven's music. Together, the words and music of this hymn combine to make one of the outstanding pieces of hymnody in the church.

> *Joyful, joyful, we adore thee,*
> *God of glory, Lord of love;*
> *Hearts unfold like flowers before thee*
> *Hail thee as the sun above.*

ℑOY TO THE WORLD
Isaac Watts, 1674 –1748

There could be no hymn which can boast of such famous parenthood as this two-hundred-fifty-year-old Christmas carol. The words were penned by that master of English hymns, that giant of sacred verse, that most famous of hymn writers, Isaac Watts. The music was composed by that wonder of divine sound, that leader of choral interpretation, that most famous of song writers George Frederick Handel (an adaption from *Messiah*). Who can say which one has been more responsible for the continued popularity of "Joy to the World"? Contemporaries, Handel died (1759) some eleven years after Watts. But what they created together has never died—and probably never will!

JUST AS I AM
Charlotte Elliott, 1789 –1871

At the age of thirty-three, Charlotte Elliott, because of the pressure of a musical education, had become a helpless invalid. She developed a bitter and rebellious spirit. One evening at her home, while being visited by Dr. Cesar Malan, a noted Swiss minister and musician, the frustrated woman inquired of the noted clergyman with despair, "How do you become a Christian?" He replied, "You pray this prayer: O God, I come to you just as I am." Fourteen years later in 1836, Miss Elliott, reminiscing about the evening with Dr. Malan, wrote her famous seven-stanza poem which began:

> *Just as I am, without one plea,*
> *But that thy blood was shed for me.*

LEAD, KINDLY LIGHT
John Henry Newman, 1801–1890

John Henry Newman, thirty-two-year-old Anglican clergyman wrote this hymn while pacing impatiently upon the deck of a becalmed, little sailing vessel bound for Marseilles with a cargo of oranges, which was stricken at the Strait of Bonifacio between the Islands of Corsica and Sardinia in June of 1833. To pass the time away during the week of waiting for the winds to fill the sails that would take them home, Newman penned the words that would mean so much to millions seeking the light of the heavenly home:

> *Lead, kindly light! amid the encircling gloom*
> *Lead Thou me on.*
> *The night is dark and I am far from home;*
> *Lead Thou me on!*
> *Keep Thou my feet;*
> *I do not ask to see*
> *The distant scene.*
> *One step enough for me.*

LEAD ON, O KING ETERNAL
Ernest W. Shurtleff, 1862–1917

This militant hymn was written for the graduating class of a theological school in 1888 by one of its members. Twenty-six-year-old Ernest W. Shurtleff wrote this hymn expressly for the graduation of his Andover Theological Seminary Class, Andover, Massachusetts. It was first publicly sung on this occasion. Little did his classmates realize as they joined in singing this remarkable hymn that they were voicing words and thoughts which would far outlive any one of them.

> *Lead on, O King Eternal,*
> *The day of march has come;*
> *Henceforth in fields of conquest*
> *Thy tents shall be our home*
> *Through days of preparation*
> *Thy grace has made us strong,*
> *And now, O King Eternal,*
> *We lift our battle song.*

LEANING ON THE EVERLASTING ARMS
Anthony Johnson Showalter, 1857–1927

A gospel hymn written in 1887 by A. J. Showalter, composer-publisher-teacher as a result of deaths in the families of two of his former pupils. While he was writing letters of consulation to them reminding them that "The Eternal God is thy refuge, and underneath are the everlasting arms," the thought occurred to him that this would be a good theme for a hymn. With the help of Elisha Hoffman, author of "Glory to His Name" and two thousand other hymn-poems, "Leaning on the Everlasting Arms" was written and published:

> *What a fellowship, what a joy divine,*
> *Leaning on the everlasting arms!*

LORD FOR TOMORROW AND ITS NEEDS
Sybil F. Partridge (Sister Mary Xavier), 1842–1910

The simple, heart-felt prayer "Lord for Tomorrow and Its Needs" was written in 1877 by a Roman Catholic nun, Sybil F. Partridge of Liverpool. Sister Mary Xavier wished to have this hymn remain anonymous, but the beauty of its words and significance of its message was too great to be hidden from Christians who would have need of its strength to sustain them in their daily tasks. The prominent American musician, Horatio R. Palmer, composed the music to this prayer.

LORD, I'M COMING HOME
William J. Kirkpatrick, 1838 –1921

One of the strangest experiences that ever occurred in the history of hymnody is related to this hymn. One evening in 1921, Professor William J. Kirkpatrick, who had written the music to "We Have Heard the Joyful Sound, Jesus Saves, Jesus Saves!" "Tis so Sweet to Trust in Jesus" and many others, told his wife that a song had been running through his mind all day and that he was going to retire to his study to put it on paper before he forgot it. Mrs. Kirkpatrick was accustomed to the fact that her husband often worked late in his study and retired for the evening thinking nothing of it. Later, after midnight, she awoke; and seeing the lights in her husband's study still burning, went in to investigate. She found him at his desk—dead! The pencil was still clutched in his lifeless hand. Spread before him were pieces of paper upon which were the lines of his newly completed hymn:

> *Coming home, coming home,*
> *Never more to roam,*
> *Open wide Thine arms of love,*
> *Lord, I'm coming home.*

Strangely enough, here was a hymn written with a dying man's last breath.

LOVE DIVINE, ALL LOVES EXCELLING
Charles Wesley, 1707–1788

Again, the immortal Reverend Charles Wesley gives the world an exaulted spiritual power in the writing of "Love Divine, All Loves Excelling." Written in 1756, it was part of his collection entitled "Hymns for Those That Seek and Those That Have Redemption in the

Blood of Jesus Christ." The first tune was written by John Zundel, noted organist in America. He served for nearly thirty years as organist of the Plymouth Church, Brooklyn, New York, where he and the famous preacher, Henry Ward Beecher, pastor of that church were intimate friends. Both their names were held in high esteem by churchgoers. The last words of this hymn, "Lost in wonder, love and praise," has been the inspiration of innumerable sermons and hymns.

Mine EYES HAVE SEEN THE GLORY or BATTLE HYMN OF THE REPUBLIC
Julia Ward Howe, 1819 –1910

In 1861 Julia Ward Howe was riding through the Union Army camps as a guest of President Lincoln. Everywhere she went the Federal troops were singing the very popular southern tune "John Brown." The catchy tune appealed to the gifted Boston writer. When she returned to her Washington hotel and tried to sleep the music stayed in her mind. Finally, she got up, and with her bathrobe still on, she wrote some words of her own to the tune:

> *"Mine eyes have seen the glory*
> *Of the coming of the Lord."*

Strangely enough, this tune which had been written originally by John W. Staffe of Richmond, Virginia, became the Union Army's marching song and was sung by the northern troops as they marched with Sherman through Richmond on their way to the sea.

More LOVE TO THEE, O CHRIST
Elizabeth Payson Prentiss, 1818 –1878

As in so many cases, this popular revival hymn, was written from the depth of great sorrow. Experience is a thorough teacher and tragedy is an unyielding instructor. Elizabeth Prentiss, author of this hymn, had lived a happy life—from the time of her birth in Portland, Maine, in 1818, through the marriage to her Presbyterian preacher husband, the Reverend George L. Prentiss, and the birth of her healthy children. But ten years after her marriage tragedy struck with a hammer blow. While in New York one child died. Soon after, the youngest child died. In a moment of despair, Mrs. Prentiss expressed her grief with a cascade of bitter tears. Her husband comforted her with the words, "In times like these God loves us all the more, just as we love our children in their distress." Later, when Mrs. Prentiss was alone, with the words of her husband still in mind, she wrote these lines:

> *More love to Thee, O Christ,*
> *More love to Thee!*
> *Hear Thou the prayer I make,*
> *On bended knee.*

My COUNTRY 'TIS OF THEE
Samuel Francis Smith, 1808 –1895

The most famous patriotic hymn in the history of America was written by a twenty-three-year-old student preparing for the Baptist ministry. In 1831, the Reverend Samuel F.

Smith, studying theology at Andover Theological Seminary, Andover, Massachusetts, penned the immortal words with the moving sentiment:

My country 'tis of thee,
Sweet land of liberty,
Of thee I sing.

MY FAITH LOOKS UP TO THEE
Ray Palmer, 1808 –1887

In the fall of 1830, just having graduated from Yale University, Ray Palmer sat down in the evening and wrote his first and finest hymn. He wrote six stanzas with such feeling and emotion that he finished the closing lines with tears streaming from his eyes. He placed it in his pocketbook and carried it around with him for two years not thinking any more about it. In the autumn of 1832, he met his good friend Dr. Lowell Mason in Boston who asked him if he knew of any new hymns that could be used in a "Hymn and Tune Book" soon to be published. Palmer, with some reluctance, gave him the words of his poem written two years previously. Mason was so impressed that he composed an original tune which he named "Olivet." Later, when Mason met Palmer, he remarked, "Mr. Palmer, you may live many years and do many good things, but I think you will be best known as the author of "My Faith Looks Up to Thee."

MY HOPE IS BUILT ON NOTHING LESS
Edward Mote, 1797–1874

Before Edward Mote became a Baptist minister in England, he was an ordinary laborer in London. Here are his words regarding the writing of his hymn, "One morning as I went to work I thought I would write a hymn on the experience of being a Christian." Before the day was finished, he had not only completed his hymn, but had sung it at a neighbor's house where much spiritual comfort was received from its content. Later, in 1836, it was published in a volume called *Hymns of Praise.*

MY JESUS I LOVE THEE
Adoniram Judson Gordon, 1836 –1895

Dr. Adoniram Judson Gordon, D. D. will be remembered as pastor of Clarendon Street Baptist Church of Boston, Massachusetts, as a founder of the famous theological college, Gordon Theological and Divinity School, Beverly Farms, Massachusetts, and as the originator of the Coronation Hymnal, but none of his accomplishments will ever equal the lasting influence of his great and touching hymn "My Jesus, I Love Thee." While preparing the Coronation Hymnal, he came across an old anonymous English hymn. Changing words and music, he gave to the world "My Jesus, I Love Thee." It is interesting to note that Dr. A. J. Gordon, a great theologian and cleric of his century and the centuries to follow, although famous for his inspired understanding of the holy scriptures, will be held in grateful reverence for the writing of a simple hymn.

NEARER MY GOD TO THEE
Sarah F. Adams, 1805 –1848

Sarah F. Adams wrote hundreds of hymns; only one was remembered! In 1841, at the request of her pastor, the Reverend William J. Fox, English Unitarian minister, Mrs. Adams wrote "Nearer My God to Thee." During a personal conversation, Fox revealed to Mrs. Adams that he was going to preach about Jacob. "Is there a hymn about Jacob's dream with which to end the service?" she is reported to have said. When Fox replied no she sat down immediately and wrote "Nearer My God to Thee." Little did she dream that this song, written so suddenly, would be so cherished by the whole world. The influence of this simple hymn is attested in part by the fact that President William McKinley requested that it be sung at his funeral and that hundreds of voices were singing these words as the great ship *Titanic* was swallowed up by the sea.

ℕOW THANK WE ALL OUR GOD
Martin Rinkart, 1586 –1649

This joyous Thanksgiving refrain was written by the Reverend Martin Rinkart, minister in the little town of Eilenburg, Saxony, at the close of the Thirty Years' War in 1648. Rinkart was the only surviving clergyman in the town, which was so crowded with refugees and so ravaged with plague and pestilence, famine and fury, that often fifty to one hundred funerals were held each day. When news finally arrived that the Peace of Westphalia had ended the great and terrible war, a decree was circulated ordering Thanksgiving services to be held in every church. Ministers were requested to preach on the text, "Now bless ye the Lord of all, who everywhere doeth great things." Martin Rinkart was so moved by the thought of this text that he sat down and wrote these words for his own Thanksgiving service:

> Now thank we all our God,
> With hearts, and hands, and voices,
> Who wondrous things hath done,
> In whom his world rejoices.

ℕOW THE DAY IS OVER
Sabine Baring-Gould, 1834 –1924

In the quaint village of Calder Valley of Yorkshire, Sabine Baring-Gould, a thirty-one-year-old curate, wrote this hymn especially for his own created "night school." The children of the valley would join in with their parents in asking Gould to tell them stories after their day's labor in the mill. Tirelessly he would tell stories and lead them in songs in his crowded two rooms. Through the chinks in the floor the voices of children would ring out the hymn written for them:

> When the morning wakens,
> Then may I arise
> Pure, and fresh, and sinless
> In Thy holy eyes.

Ⓞ BROTHER MAN,
FOLD TO THY HEART THY BROTHER
John Greenleaf Whittier, 1807–1892

John Greenleaf Whittier believed in the simplicity of worship and felt that the true worship of man, recognized by God, is when he loves others. In 1848 he wrote a poem entitled "Worship" based on James 1:27: "Pure religion and undefiled before God and the Father is this, To visit the fatherless and widows in their affliction, and to keep himself unspotted from the world." From this poem developed one of the church's finer brotherhood hymns:

> O brother man, fold to thy heart thy brother;
> Where pity dwells, the peace of God is there;
> To worship rightly is to love each other,
> Each smile a hymn, each kindly deed a prayer.

COME ALL YE FAITHFUL
author unknown

One of the most popular Christmas hymns, "O Come All Ye Faithful" might never have been known by the English-speaking world if it had not been for the chance work of a wandering scribe. In 1750, John Francis Wade, who made his way in life as a professional copy writer, included an "original" Christmas poem, called "Adeste Fideles" in a manuscript compiled for the English Roman Catholic College at Lisbon, Portugal. Thirty-five years later a copy of the hymn was sent to the Portuguese Chapel in London, from which its popularity spread throughout the world. Many critics say that Wade "borrowed" the words and tune of this beautiful nativity hymn from an old French chorale. But, whether or not Wade originated the hymn, the fact that he included it in the manuscript copied for the Catholic College in Lisbon has meant that the world received one of its most loved Christmas songs. "O Come All Ye Faithful" received its title from a translation into English by Frederick Oakley, an English canon, in 1852.

COME, O COME EMMANUEL
author unknown

A twelfth-century Latin hymn popular during the Advent Season, translated into English during the middle nineteenth century by the Reverend John M. Neale. The Latin hymn was used originally as a short musical response to be sung at vesper services. The song tells us that Advent is a joyous season because it is the time when God draws near to everyone to deliver them from bondage with the coming of Emmanuel.

> O come, O come, Emmanuel,
> And ransom captive Israel,
> That mourns in lonely exile here
> Until the Son of God appear.

DAY OF REST AND GLADNESS
Christopher Wordsworth, 1807–1885

Classified as a teaching hymn, "O Day of Rest and Gladness" was written in 1862 by Christopher Wordsworth, nephew of the famed English poet Wordsworth. Young Wordsworth was serving as country parish minister at the time, but was later appointed bishop of Lincoln. This hymn is one of the most outstanding examples of the meaning and purpose of the Sabbath that can be found in the history of hymnody.

> O day of rest and gladness,
> O day of joy and light,
> O balm of care and sadness,
> Most beautiful, most bright;
> On Thee, the high and lowly,
> Through ages joined in tune,
> Sing Holy, Holy, Holy
> To the great God Triune.

FOR A CLOSER WALK WITH GOD
William Cowper, 1731–1800

The son of a clergyman, William Cowper, was born at Berkhampstead, Hertfordshire, England, on November 15, 1731, and lived for sixty-nine years. The burden of his mental affliction and at times partial insanity was lightened by his desire and ability to write. Most of his hymns were written when he resided with his fellow hymnist John Newton in Olney, and at one time they issued a volume of hymns under the title, "Olney Hymns." This suffering man was loved by many and known to be a true Christian. He was able to produce some of our sweetest and most spiritual hymns such as:

> *O for a closer walk with God,*
> *A calm and heavenly frame;*
> *A light to shine upon the road*
> *That leads me to the Lamb.*

FOR A THOUSAND TONGUES TO SING
Charles Wesley, 1707–1788

Charles Wesley wrote this hymn on the first anniversary of his conversion to God, which occurred on Sunday, May 21, 1738. It is said that the opening lines came as a result of a conversation between Wesley and Peter Bohler, the Moravian. On the subject of praising Christ, Bohler had said, "Had I a thousand tongues I would praise Him with them all." From this chance remark Wesley conceived the idea of this hymn.

> *O for a thousand tongues to sing*
> *My great Redeemer's praise,*
> *The glories of my God and King,*
> *The triumphs of His grace!*
> *My gracious Master and my God,*
> *Assist me to proclaim,*
> *To spread thro' all the earth abroad*
> *The honors of Thy name.*

GOD, OUR HELP IN AGES PAST
Isaac Watts, 1674 –1748

This international hymn written by one of the greatest hymn masters, Isaac Watts, leads the list as a favorite of many Christians. It was written early in the eighteenth century and its words have been a comfort to many in moments of crisis. It is universal in appeal and lends celestial beauty and strength through its words:

> *A thousand ages in Thy sight*
> *Are like an evening gone;*
> *Short as the watch that ends the night*
> *Before the rising sun.*

The original title "Our God, Our Help in Ages Past" was substituted with "O God, Our Help in Ages Past," by John Wesley in 1738.

HOLY NIGHT
Adolphe Adam, 1803 –1856

A beautiful, haunting French carol whose melody was written by Adolphe Adam, composer born in Paris in 1803. A story is told that on Christmas Eve in 1870 during the Franco-Prussian War, the French and German soldiers were facing one another in opposite trenches. Suddenly a young French soldier leaped from his trench and startled the Germans by singing in a loud, clear voice, the "Cantique de Noel" or "O Holy Night." The Germans were so surprised that not a shot was fired. Not to be outdone, a German soldier stepped forward and sang Luther's "From Heaven Above to Earth I Come."

LITTLE TOWN OF BETHLEHEM
Phillips Brooks, 1835 –1893

The dramatic birth of this popular Christmas hymn was as sudden as the announcement of the angelic host, concerning the birth of Christ, to the shepherds in the fields outside Bethlehem. The seeds of the hymn were sown in 1865 when on Christmas Eve in Bethlehem, Phillips Brooks, noted Episcopal bishop, attended services in the ancient basilica claimed to have been built by Emperor Constantine in the fourth century. He was a young minister at the time, and the beauty of the simple service made a permanent impression on his heart. Three years later, while rector of Holy Trinity Church, Philadelphia, at the request of the children of the Church School, Phillips Brooks wrote a new Christmas song. His trip to the Holy Land came back to mind vividly and he penned these beautiful words:

> "O little town of Bethlehem,
> How still we see thee lie."

The thought of the little town of Bethlehem was so strong in his mind, that Brooks completed the entire hymn in one evening. The next day when Lewis Redner, organist and church school superintendent, came into his study, Phillip Brooks gave him the poem and asked if he could write some music for it so that it could be sung during the Christmas Season. Redner waited for inspiration, but none came. On the night before Christmas he woke up suddenly, in the middle of the night, the melody of the song ringing in his ears like happy bells. Seizing the nearest piece of paper, he wrote down the music that was so clear in his mind and went back to sleep. In the morning he harmonized the melody, and that same day the little children of Holy Trinity Church sang for the first time one of the most loved Christmas carols.

LOVE THAT WILT NOT LET ME GO
George Matheson, 1842–1906

This great hymn of courage and faith was written, strangely enough, under circumtances of tragic inner conflict and severe mental suffering as a release from personal tragedy. Dr. George Matheson, beloved clergyman in the Church of Scotland, and totally blind since the age of fifteen, composed this strong hymn in 1882. The courage and fortitude of Dr. Matheson was evidenced by the dramatic fact that from this deep sorrow and heartache he could write:

> O love that wilt not let me go,
> I rest my weary soul in thee.

MASTER, LET ME WALK WITH THEE
Washington Gladden, 1836 –1918

Dr. Washington Gladden did not think of himself as a hymn writer; yet in 1879 he wrote a poem for the publication *Sunday Afternoon*, which has become one of the world's most cherished devotional hymns.

> O Master, let me walk with Thee
> In lowly paths of service free;
> Tell me thy secret; help me to bear
> The strain of toil, the fret of care.

his hymn reflected Gladden's religious philosophy which was in a sentence, "Religion is nothing but friendship; friendship with God and with man." It is no wonder that his hymn was found such a warm response.

 ## ONCE TO EVERY MAN AND NATION
James Russell Lowell, 1819 –1891

In 1845, at the same time Abraham Lincoln was opposing in Congress the agitators for a war with Mexico, the famed poet James Russell Lowell was usng his talent to speak out against what he thought was the plan of the slave-holding states to gain more territory. It was a ninety-line poem, later reduced to thirty-two lines, which became one of the strongest hymns challenging national righteousness ever printed:

> Once to every man and nation
> Comes the moment to decide,
> In the strife of truth with falsehood,
> For the good or evil side.

Legend says that the tune used for his hymn can be traced back to its discovery in a bottle washed up on the shores of Wales.

 ## ONWARD CHRISTIAN SOLDIERS
Sabine Baring-Gould, 1834 –1924

"Onward Christian Soldiers," written in 1865 by the Reverend Sabine Baring-Gould an English clergyman, is one of the most popular hymns ever composed for children. It was created originally as a processional for singing Sunday school children marching between villages. It is said that Baring-Gould was deeply disappointed in what he considered many of its imperfections and never imagined that it would reach the height of popularity that it later attained. A humorous incident is reported concerning the last line of the hymn. Many objected to the children's carrying processional crosses while they were marching—in a moment of whimsy, the last line "going on before" was changed to "left behind the door." "Onward Christian Soldiers" is, without doubt, the greatest marching hymn of all Christendom.

 ## O SACRED HEAD NOW WOUNDED
Bernard of Clairvaux, 1091–1153

The theme of "O Sacred Head Now Wounded" had its origin in the solitude of a lonely monk's cell in the mind of Bernard of Clairvaux, famous twelfth-century monk. The story of this medieval monk is one of the most beautiful and romantic of all times. So wonderful was his spirit and leadership that the monastery that first housed only eleven monks, increased to one hundred twenty-five. A dedicated person, St. Bernard refused many high posts in the church and continued on as Abbott of Clairvaux. It was in his cell that he would meditate upon the suffering of the Savior on the cross, and penned the Passion hymn, which is used particularly for Passion Sunday. It was first translated into German from the Latin by Paul Gerhart in 1656. Then later for the Anglican Church, by Dr. James W. Alexander, in 1830.

 ## O WORSHIP THE KING, ALL GLORIOUS ABOVE
Robert Grant, 1779 –1838

One day in the 1830s approximately eight years before his death, Sir Robert Grant, who became governor of Bombay in 1834, was glancing through the Anglo-German Psalter written in 1561. He was greatly impressed and inspired by a translation of Psalm 104 by William Kethe. Immediately he began to write an original poem about the omnipotence of God, guided by the theme of the classic Hebrew psalm.

> O worship the King, all glorious above,
>   O gratefully sing His power and His love;
> Our Shield and Defender, the Ancient of Days,
>   Pavilioned in splendor, and girded with praise.

It received public acclaim in 1833, when it was first published in Bickersteth's *Christian Psalmody.* The tune most frequently used is called "Lyons," an adaptation from Johann M. Haydn.

ℙASS ME NOT, O GENTLE SAVIOR
Fanny J. Crosby, 1820 –1915

If ever a hymn writer used a theme which was indicative of his or her life, it was the blind Fanny Crosby when she wrote, in 1868, "Pass Me Not, O Gentle Savior." Of a truth, God certainly did not pass her by. She turned a tragedy at six weeks of age into a triumph of a lifetime. She overcame a terrible, personal adversity and contributed a life of power and purpose to the world. Fanny Jane Crosby was a little baby girl of six weeks, in May, 1820, when she caught a common cold. A country doctor of Putnam County, New York, unwittingly prescribed a hot mustard poltice. She was blinded for life!

When she was five sympathetic neighbors and friends pooled their money and sent her to a noted New York surgeon, Dr. Valentine Mott. After a careful examination, the specialist said sadly that there was nothing he could do. Looking toward her, he said, "Poor little blind girl!" Fanny Crosby always remembered these words and turned the sympathetic remark of a kindly physician into the purposeful pattern of a truly remarkable personality. The world may have thought of her as the "poor little blind girl," but not Fanny Crosby! She once told a friend that her blindness had proved a blessing, because it enabled her to be more alone where the writing of her poetry became easy. And she told another that if she had a choice she still would remain blind, for when she died the first face she ever would see would be the face of her "blessed Savior."

> Savior, Savior,
> Hear my humble cry;
> While on others Thou art calling,
> Do not pass me by.

ℙRAISE TO THE LORD, THE ALMIGHTY
Joachim Neander, 1650 –1680

This hymn of praise was written by Joachim Neander shortly before his death at thirty years of age in 1680, in Bremen, Germany, the city of his birth. It is said that the hymn developed out of a difficult situation experienced in Dusseldorf in the Rhineland, Germany, while he was schoolmaster there. When Neander refused to conform with the rules of the elders of the Reformed Church who controlled the school, he was forced to seek retreat in a wild cave where this and many other poems were written.

> Praise to the Lord, the Almighty,
>   the King of creation!
> O my soul, praise him,
>   for he is thy health and salvation! All ye who hear,
> Now to his temple draw near;
> Join me in glad adoration!

REJOICE, THE LORD IS KING
Charles Wesley, 1707–1788

One of the six favorite hymns of Charles Wesley. The great Methodist hymn writer compiled thousands of hymns during his lifetime of eighty-one years and this one was written somewhere in the vicinity of 1750. It is difficult to realize that one man could write such all-time favorites as "Jesus Lover of My Soul," "Love Divine All Loves Excelling," "O for a Thousand Tongues to Sing," "O Thou Who Comest from Above," "Ye Servants of God," and "Rejoice, the Lord Is King." But he did, and many, many others. Perhaps it suffices to say that here was a man so filled with the joy of the Spirit of God that it continuously manifestered itself with the glad sound of music and psalm!

REJOICE YE PURE IN HEART
Edward Hayes Plumptre, 1821–1891

In May 1865 a great choir festival was held in Peterborough Cathedral in England. A new and stirring hymn, written especially for the festival by the Reverend Edward Hayes Plumptre, was introduced:

> Rejoice ye pure in heart,
> Rejoice, give thanks and sing:
> Your glorious banner wave on high,
> The cross of Christ your King.

RESCUE THE PERISHING
Fanny J. Crosby, 1820 –1915

In 1869, Fanny Crosby wrote the words for "Rescue the Perishing" while riding between Brooklyn and the Bowery in a hired horse-drawn hack. She had just attended a service in the Bowery Mission where she had been asked to address an audience made up of New York's lower derelicts. While traveling home after the service the blind poetess' mind could not help dwelling upon the experience through which she had just passed. Lines of a poem began to form in her mind. Before she reached her home the poem was completed and a new hymn was born.

> Rescue the perishing
> Care for the dying,
> Snatch them from pity from sin and the grave;
> Weep o'er the erring one,
> Lift up the fallen,
> Tell them of Jesus the Mighty to save.

RIDE ON, RIDE ON IN MAJESTY
Henry Hart Milman, 1791–1868

The hymn, "Ride On, Ride On in Majesty" is the most well-known of the Palm Sunday hymns. It was written by the Reverend Henry Hart Milman, dean of St. Paul's in London. Dean Milman, born in 1791, also won world acclaim as a historian. The Reverend John Bacchus Dykes wrote the music to this hymn and was famous in his own right for such favorites as "Lead, Kindly Light," and "Ten Thousand Times Ten Thousand."

> Ride on, ride on in majesty!
> Hark! all the tribes Hosanna cry;
> O Savior meek, pursue thy road,
> With palms and scattered garments strewed.

RISE UP, O MEN OF GOD

William Pierson Merrill, 1867–1954

In 1911, William Pierson Merrill was aboard a Lake Michigan steamer on his way to Chicago. As he watched the waves lapping around the boat, he thought of a remark made to him by Nolan R. Best, an editor, just a short while before, "What we need, Dr. Merrill, is a good brotherhood hymn!" Suddenly the words came to him, quickly and without any effort he wrote them down:

> Rise up, O men of God!
> Have done with lesser things;
> Give heart and mind and soul and strength
> To serve the King of Kings.

Immediately the hymn was widely acclaimed and developed the reputation as a hymn that challenged men to do something, and to do it without delay.

ROCK OF AGES

Augustus Montague Toplady, 1740 –1778

The writing of "Rock of Ages" by the Reverend Augustus M. Toplady, an English vicar in 1775, is one of the strangest stories in the history of hymns. The words, "Rock of ages, cleft for me,/Let me hide myself in thee;/Let the water and the blood,/From thy riven side which flowed,/Be of sin the double cure,/Save from wrath and make me pure," were first written on the back side of a playing card, the six of diamonds. It came about one day when Toplady was walking some distance from his home and was caught in a sudden, violent storm. There was no shelter nearby, but the vicar spied a huge cleft running down a ledge beside the road. He took refuge here and was protected from the storm. He thought, while there, of the spiritual significance of his experience. God is a refuge from the storms of life. Reaching down to the ground, he picked up a playing card, which he found lying there, and upon this surface, the famous words were penned.

> Rock of ages, cleft for me,
> Let me hide myself in thee;
> Let the water and the blood,
> From thy riven side which flowed,
> Be of sin the double cure,
> Save from wrath and make me pure.

SAFE IN THE ARMS OF JESUS

Fanny J. Crosby, 1820 –1915

One of Fanny Crosby's most popular hymns, it was written in less than thirty minutes, at the request of William H. Doane who had composed a new tune to be used at a Sunday School Convention in Cincinnati in 1868. Doane, trying to catch a train to the Convention, had rushed in to Fanny Crosby's home, requesting words for his new tune. Hurriedly he played the tune for her, saying with impatience that he had only thirty-five minutes to catch his train. Fanny Crosby listened intently while he played, and said at the conclusion without hesitation. "Your tune is saying, "safe in the arms of Jesus." In a matter of minutes she had penned these famous lines:

> Safe in the arms of Jesus,
> Safe on his gentle breast;
> There by his love o'ershaded,
> Sweetly my soul shall rest.

SAVED BY GRACE

Fanny J. Crosby, 1820 –1915

A gospel hymn written in 1894 by Fanny J. Crosby, one of hymnody's most dramatic authors. Ira D. Sankey, D. L. Moody's song leader, lists this hymn as one of his five favorites to sing as solos. It was first heard by the public, as a recitation by Miss Crosby, at a summer conference in Northfield, Massachusetts, conducted by Dr. Adoniram Judson Gordon in 1894. An English reporter was present and requested a copy to take to London, where it was published in his paper. Sankey discovered the poem in the English paper and requested George C. Stebbins, famed gospel tunesmith, to compose music for it. Not only did this hymn remain one of Sankey's favorites during his lifetime, but it became the favorite of hundreds of thousands throughout the world.

> *And I shall see him face to face,*
> *And tell the story, saved by grace.*
> *And I shall see him face to face,*
> *And tell the story, saved by grace.*

SAVIOR, AGAIN TO THY DEAR NAME WE RAISE
John Ellerton, 1826 –1893

This majestic church hymn was written in a moment of inspiration by the Reverend John Ellerton, an English vicar, in 1866. He was responsible for providing the hymn at the annual Hymn Festival held in Cheshire. On the night before, Ellerton seized his last Sunday's sermon and scribbled these words on the back:

> *Savior, again to thy dear name we raise*
> *With one accord our parting hymn of praise;*
> *We stand to blee thee 'ere our worship cease;*
> *And now, departing, wait thy word of peace.*

Ellerton's hastily penned hymn proved to be one of the most popular that he wrote and was translated into many languages.

SAVIOR LIKE A SHEPHERD LEAD US
Dorothy Ann Thrupp, 1779 –1847

In 1859 William D. Bradbury gave the Christian world the great and peaceful hymn "Savior Like A Shepherd Lead Us." It is believed that this hymn poem had been written by the Reverend Henry F. Lyte, author of "Abide with Me," while others say it first appeared in a book by Dorothy Ann Thrupp. Bradbury was a protege of the talented religious composer Lowell Mason and was instrumental in influencing and encouraging blind Fanny Crosby to turn her talents from writing secular songs to hymns for the church. Though poverty-stricken in his childhood, he was able to contribute great wealth through his immortal music to such hymn poems as "Just as I Am," "Sweet Hour of Prayer," and "He Leadeth Me."

SAVIOR THY DYING LOVE
Sylvanus Dryden Phelps, 1816 –1895

This hymn of consecration was written in 1862 by Dr. S. Dryden Phelps, an American Baptist minister. Published in Sankey's *Gospel Hymns* under the title "Something for

Jesus," the music was written by another prominent American Baptist clergyman, Robert Lowry, in 1872. On his seventieth birthday Dr. Phelps received a telegram from Lowry which expressed the sentiment of all who knew him, "It is worth living seventy years, even if nothing comes of it but one such hymn as this one. Happy is the man who can produce one song which the world will keep on singing after its author shall have passed away."

> Savior, thy dying love, thou gavest me;
> Nor should I aught withhold,
> Dear Lord, from thee;
> In love my soul would bow,
> My heart fulfill its vow,
> Some off'ring bring thee now,
> Something for thee.

SHALL WE GATHER AT THE RIVER
Robert Lowry, 1826 –1899

Dr. Robert Lowry wrote this "Hymn of the Hereafter" as the result of a raging epidemic, July, 1864, in Brooklyn, New York. He had just accepted a call to the Baptist Church of Brooklyn. It was an unusually hot and humid summer. When the eidemic struck hundreds were left dead and dying in its wake. Everwhere Lowry went comforting his people he heard the words, "Pastor, we have parted at the river of death; shall we meet again at the river of life?" Filled with this thought, Lowry wrote down the words:

> Shall we gather at the river,
>   Where bright angel feet have trod,
> With its crystal tide forever
>   Flowing by the throne of God?

SILENT NIGHT, HOLY NIGHT
Joseph Mohr, 1792–1848

This most beautiful of Christmas hymns was written on the night before Christmas in 1818 at the little village of Oberndorf, Austria, by Joseph Mohr, the vicar of the Church of St. Nicholas. Mohr gave the words of the simple poem to his organist Franz Gruber, who composed the music in time for the Christmas Eve service. The drama of the first rendition of "Silent Night, Holy Night" was augmented by the fact that the organ broke down, and the first public presentation of Christmas' most famous hymn was a simple duet between the author and the composer with voice and plain guitar accompaniment. The breaking down of the organ was instrumental in popularizing the new hymn. Later when the organ was being repaired, Gruber played the new carol on it as a means of testing the tone of the instrument. The repairman was fascinated and enchanted. He requested a copy and took it back with him to his own village of Zillerthal where it was received joyously. Four daughters of a Zillerthal glove maker named Strasse used this song in concerts from town to town and village to village while their father sold gloves. Soon everyone was singing "Silent Night, Holy Night," and so they have through the generations up to now, and so they will as long as Christmas is a part of the human life.

SING THEM OVER AGAIN TO ME
Philip Paul Bliss, 1838 –1876

"Sing Them Over Again to Me," a popular gospel hymn, also called "Wonderful Words of Life," with words and music written by Philip P. Bliss in the middle nineteenth century. Although it is classified in that group of hymns considered by most critics as being sentimental" or "emotional" it has been well received by congregations who love to sing songs with spirit and feeling. Philip Bliss, born in 1838, was the author of many gospel hymns similar to "Wonderful Words of Life," including "Let the Lower Lights Be Burning" and "I Am So Glad That Jesus Loves Me."

SOFTLY AND TENDERLY
Will L. Thompson, 1847–1909

When the famed evangelist Dwight L. Moody lay dying, Will Thompson, the author and composer of "Softly and Tenderly," visited him to give spiritual strength in his hour of greatest need. Taking the composer's hand in his own Moody said, "Will, I would rather have written 'Softly and Tenderly,' than anything I have been able to do in my whole life." They were prophetic words, for this most famous composition of Will Lamartine Thompson the "Bard of Ohio" has been one of the "all-time" influential hymns of history. It's tender words have reached more needy hearts than almost any other:

> Softly and tenderly Jesus is calling,
> Calling for you and for me.

SOFTLY NOW THE LIGHT OF DAY
George Washington Doane, 1799 –1859

Bishop George Washington Doane, famed Episcopal clergyman, was twenty-five years old when he wrote "Softly Now the Light of Day" in 1824. Originally titled "Evening" the author had these words to say concerning the writing of his hymn-poem: "Let my prayer be set forth before Thee as incense; and the lifting up of my hands as the evening sacrifice."

> Softly now the light of day
> Fades upon my sight away;
> Free from care, from labor free,
> Lord, I would commune with Thee.
> Thou, whose all-pervading eye
> Naught escapes, without, within,
> Pardon each infirmity
> Open fault, and secret sin.

SOLDIERS OF CHRIST ARISE
Charles Wesley, 1707–1788

Charles Wesley was one of the master hymn writers. "Soldiers of Christ Arise" was one of the master hymns of Christian action. Written in 1749, it was first published in a book called "Hymns and Sacred Poems" under the title of "The Whole Armour of God." Based on the text Ephesians 6:10-17, this martial hymn with the spiritual connotation is a challenging admonition to wrestle against the powers of evil with the weapons of full faith and certain knowledge that the power of God is invincible. Wesley's gift of inspiring action in Christian living is unmatched by the hymnwriters of all time.

> Soldiers of Christ, arise, And put your armor on,
> Strong in the strength which God supplies
>   Through his eternal Son;
> Strong in the Lord of hosts,
>   And in His mighty power,
> Who in the strength of Jesus trusts
>   Is more than conqueror.

SPIRIT OF GOD, DESCEND UPON MY HEART

George Croly, 1780 –1860

"Spirit of God, Descend upon My Heart" was written by an Irish priest George Croly who was born in 1780 and lived to be eighty years old. The original title to this hymn was "Holiness Desired." It is interesting to note that any ten-syllable tune is adaptable to this hymn. This comforting words and reassuring faith, stressed especially in the second the third verses make this hymn a favorite.

> *I ask no dream, no prophet ecstasies.*
> *No sudden rending of the veil of clay,*
> *No angel visitant, no opening skies;*
> *But take the dimness of my soul away.*
> *Hast thou not bid me love thee, God and King?*
> *All, all thine own—soul, heart, and strength, and*
> *mind.*

STAND UP, STAND UP FOR JESUS

George R. Duffield, 1818 –1888

This famous church hymn, one of the outstanding men's choruses ever written, originated as a result of the dramatic and unusual death of the Reverend Dudley A. Tyng, a young Episcopalian minister of Philadelphia in 1858. In a letter dated May 29, 1883, Dr. Geroge Duffield, author of the hymn, revealed to a friend the unusual occurence that led to the writing of "Stand Up, Stand Up for Jesus." Duffield heard Tyng preach to a Young Men's Christian Association group on the text of Exodus referring to the "slain of the Lord." Within one week Tyng himself had been slain and the hymn had been written. The Wednesday following Tyng's sermon, the young Episcopalian had gone into the barn where a mule was pulling on a wheel-power corn-shelling machine. Patting the mule's neck, Tyng's sleeve caught in the cogs of the wheel and his arm was completely severed from his body. Within two hours he was dead. The following Sunday Duffield, using the dramatic death as an illustration, preached on the text in Ephesians 6:11 which speaks of putting on the whole armor of God and standing in the truth. He closed his sermon with the words he had written the previous Friday which had been inspired by Tung's tragic death:

> *Stand up, stand up for Jesus,*
> *Ye soldiers of the cross.*

STILL, STILL WITH THEE
WHEN PURPLE MORNING BREAKETH

Harriet Beecher Stowe, 1812–1896

This beautiful morning hymn based on Psalm 139:18 was written in the middle nineteenth century by Harriet Beecher Stowe, author of *Uncle Tom's Cabin*. Although Mrs. Stowe wrote a number of hymns this one proved to be the most popular. The tune is taken from Felix Mendelssohn's collection of forty-eight pieces known as "Song Without Words."

> *Still, still with thee*
> *When purple morning breaketh,*

When the bird waketh,
And the shadows flee;
Fairer then morning,
Lovelier than daylight,
Dawns the sweet consciousness,
I am with thee.

$\mathfrak{S}$UN OF MY SOUL, THOU SAVIOR DEAR

John Keble, 1792–1866

This hymn, written by John Keble in 1820, was part of a famed collection of hymn and poems entitled *The Christian Year* which sold over 300,000 copies in forty-six years. Based on Luke 24:29 the hymn represents a lone traveler, after sundown, continuing his darkened way in the trust and confidence that God will take care for his needs. The simple, delightful sincerity of the hymn has made it a favorite through the years.

$\mathfrak{S}$UNSET AND EVENING STAR

Alfred Lord Tennyson, 1809 –1892

Sunset and evening star,
  And one clear call for me,
And may there be no moaning of the bar
  When I put out to sea,
For though from out our bourne of time and place
  The flood may bear me far,
I hope to see my Pilot face to face
  When I have crossed the bar.

It was the immortal English poet, Alfred Lord Tennyson who penned this sublime prayer three years before his death. The deep sense of real "Presence" was characterized in all his mature spiritual life and such faith made no room for dying terrors. His prayer was answered, for his death was serene and dreadless. His "Pilot" guided him gently "across the bar."

$\mathfrak{S}$WEET BY AND BY

Sanford Filmore Bennett, 1836 –1898

It is said that this entire hymn, including words by S. F. Bennett and music by J. P. Webster, was written and composed in less than thirty minutes. Webster, who was subject to moods of melancholy and depression, once visited his friend Bennett who was writing at his desk. Walking to the fire, Webster turned his back to his friend without a word. When Bennett asked him what the matter was, he received the curt reply that "it would be alright, by and by." Seizing upon the last three words Bennett exclaimed, "The sweet by and by! That would make a good title for a hymn!" Whereupon, he wrote without stopping, covering the paper as fast as his pen could go. When he finished he handed the manuscript to Webster, who immediately sat down and composed a melody to fit the stirring words. From this union in the village of Elkhorn, Wisconsin, almost a hundred years ago, the gospel hymn was born:

There's a land that is fairer than day
  And by faith we can see it afar,
For the Father waits, over the way,
  To prepare us a dwelling-place there.

SWEET HOUR OF PRAYER
William W. Walford, 1800 –1875 (approximate dates)

"Sweet Hour of Prayer," one of the world's most popular prayer hymns, was written by a man who could not see. In 1842, the Reverend William W. Walford, a blind English clergyman, dictated his inspirational poem of prayer to the Reverend Thomas Salmon, minister at the Congregational Church, Coleshill, England. Salmon took it with him on a journey to New York City, where it was pubished in September 1845. Without doubt, Walford's physical blindness gave him a spiritual sight to see, where many others could not see the tremendous significance of the power of illumination in prayer.

TAKE MY LIFE AND LET IT BE
Frances Ridley Havergal, 1836 –1879

This challenging gospel hymn was written by Frances Ridley Havergal in 1874, four years before her death. The words were conceived while visiting the home of a friend where the author helped convert ten people. She was so happy and excited that she could not sleep until the words which were forming in her mind were written down. Throughout her life, Miss Havergall considered this hymn a measure of her own consecration to God and constantly reviewed the verses to renew her own spiritual life.

> *Take my life and let it be*
> *Consecrated, Lord, to thee;*
> *Take my moments and my days,*
> *Let them flow in ceaseless praise.*

TAKE TIME TO BE HOLY
William Dunn Longstaff, 1822–1894

Although "Take Time to Be Holy" was written by an Englishman, William Dunn Longstaff, after listening to a sermon on the text, "Be ye holy; for I am holy," it was an American musician, George Stebbins who brought it into being. Stebbins, who was at one time choir leader in Tremont Temple, Boston, Massachusetts, and who wrote the music for such hymns as "True-Hearted, Whole-Hearted," "Jesus Is Tenderly Calling," "Have Thine Own Way, Lord," and many, many more for such hymn writers as Frances Havergal, Adelaide Pollard and Fanny Crosby, was in India in the autumn of 1890 when someone mentioned the need for a hymn on holiness. Stebbins remembered a poem on the subject by William Longstaff which he had cut out and saved. He searched among his papers, found it, and set the stanzas to music. Thus in distant India, "Take Time to Be Holy" began a popular career that has continued in every generation.

THE CHURCH'S ONE FOUNDATION
Samuel John Stone, 1839 –1900

Bishop Gray was the one who stirred Samuel John Stone, born in 1839, then a curate at Windsor, to write the hymn "The Church's One Foundation." Bishop Gray was defending the name of Bishop Colenso of Natal whose name stood for heresy and disloyalty. His treatment of the atonement and the sacraments were considered unorthodox. It is claimed that Bishop Colenso was before his time. Is it not ironic that the great hymn that his "heresies" inspired has become a magnificent statement about the church?

> The Church's one foundation
> Is Jesus Christ her Lord;
> She is his new creation
> By water and the word.
> From heaven he came and sought her
> To be his holy bride;
> With his own blood He bought her,
> And for her life he died.

THE GOD OF ABRAHAM PRAISE

Daniel Ben Judah, fourteenth century

This fourteenth-century Hebrew melody was written by Daniel Ben Judah. Although it has been translated from the original many times, it is based on the Hebrew Yigdal or Doxology which is part of the morning and evening ritual of Jewish worship. In 1770, Thomas Oliver, a Methodist minister, while attending a Synagogue service in London, heard the haunting Hebrew tune for the first time. Its depth of beauty in the minor key enraptured him so completely that he was inspired immediately to secure it for Christian worship. After acquiring the tune he wrote the stanzas of "The God of Abraham Praise," and it has been used widely as a recessional and processional hymn through the years:

> The God of Abraham praise,
> All praised be his name,
> Who was, and is, and is to be,
> And still the same!
> The one eternal God,
> Ere aught that now appears;
> The First, the Last: beyond all thought
> His timeless years!

THE LIGHT OF THE WORLD IS JESUS

Philip Paul Bliss, 1838 –1876

In the summer of 1875 P. P. Bliss was passing through the hall of his room in his home at Chicago, Illinois, when the words and music of this favorite gospel hymn came to his mind in sudden inspiration. Immediately he sat down and wrote the hymn as the Spirit spoke in his heart. As has happened so many times in the experience of hymn writers the complete song, melody, harmony, and words were written in a matter of moments—as if the Spirit himself was guiding the hand that penned the immortal phrases.

THE MORNING LIGHT IS BREAKING

Samuel Francis Smith, 1808 –1895

Samuel Francis Smith was twenty-four years old at the time Adoniram Judson, one of the first famous five missionaries from Tabernacle Congregational Church, Salem, Massachusetts, commissioned by the American Board for Foreign Missions, was dramatically active in Burma. Smith was so stirred by reports being sent back to the home church that he wrote this hymn which has been a favorite of missionaries ever since:

> The morning light is breaking,
> The darkness disappears;
> The sons of earth are waking
> To penitential tears;

Each breeze that sweeps the ocean
Brings tidings from afar
Of nations in commotion,
Prepared for Zion's war.

Some years later, one of Smith's own sons went to Burma as a missionary.

THE NINETY AND NINE
Elizabeth Clephane, 1830 –1869

It is said of this hymn that it is the only one in hymnody written and composed while the author was singing it to the congregation for the first time. The great evangelist Dwight L. Moody was conducting services in Edinburgh, Scotland. The equally famed song leader Ira David Sankey was responsible for the song leading and solos during the services. While riding on the train with Moody from Glasgow to Edinburgh, Sankey spotted a little poem in the local paper written by a Scottish girl named Elizabeth Clephane. He tore the poem out and stuck it in his pocket. Now at the opening service in Edinburg, it was time for Sankey's solo. Moody's sermon subject was the Good Shepherd but Sankey had not been told and had no appropriate song. He had not even planned to sing alone. Suddenly he thought of the poem in his pocket. It fitted the theme of Moody's sermon perfectly. But there was no music! Quickly, in a seizure of inspiration Sankey whipped out the poem, placed it on the piano, and composed the music, note for note as it is today, singing for the very first time as he composed.

THERE IS A FOUNTAIN FILLED WITH BLOOD
William Cowper, 1731–1800

William Cowper was born in 1731 and lived to the edge of the nineteenth century. He was a strange man driven by deep and emotional phobias. Four times he was committed to insane asylums; many times he attempted suicide. His sixty-nine years of life were physical torture and mental anguish. However, there was one bright spot in this holocaust of torture—the peaceful home of the Reverend John Newton. Newton, who wrote hundreds of hymns, provided a place where Cowper could write his literary masterpieces. When Cowper spoke, his words were twisted and impaired by lisping and stammering; but when he wrote they tumbled forth shining cataracts of verbal beauty. It was here in this haven, the home of Newton, that Cowper wrote "There Is a Fountain Filled with Blood." Hundreds of people have sung this grand old favorite through the years. Probably unaware of the struggle Cowper had in his life, they see only the beauty and feeling reflected in this hymn. God truly "works in mysterious ways his wonders to perform."

THERE IS A GREEN HILL FAR AWAY
Cecil F. Alexander, 1818 –1895

This hymn, picturing the crucifixion of Jesus, was written in 1848 by Mrs. Cecil Frances Alexander, wife of the Reverend W. Alexander, D.D., bishop of Derry, Ireland. Written for children with the purpose of making the Scripture more understandable, Mrs. Alexander conceived the idea for the song while driving on a shopping expedition to Derry. Outside the city walls there was a little green-covered hill which always made her think of Calvary. Therefore, when she explained the meaning of the death and resurrection of Christ, this little hill came into mind and she wrote:

There is a green hill far away
Without a city wall.

THERE'S A WIDENESS IN GOD'S MERCY
Frederick William Faber, 1814 –1863

It was said of Frederick William Faber, Anglican clergyman, the author of this hymn, that his vivid, unusual imagination was almost without comparison. "There's a Wideness in God's mercy" written probably in 1846 is a good example of his remarkable talent. Comparing God's love to the wideness of the sea demonstrates not only an extraordinary ability to choose the right metaphor, but a deep insight in the boundlessness of the mercy of the Almighty. This hymn was one of one hundred and fifty written by Faber, all of them composed after he was converted to Roman Catholicism in 1846. Protestants have used his hymns freely, however, finding in them a true expression of living faith.

> *There's a wideness in God's mercy*
> *Like the wideness of the sea.*

THIS IS MY FATHER'S WORLD
Maltbie Davenport Babcock, 1858 –1901

One of hymnody's most beautiful nature poems, this hymn was written by the Reverend Maltbie D. Babcock, prominent Presbyterian minister, during his first pastorate in Lockport, New York. Filled with a deep devotion to his calling, the learned clergyman would often say to his people, "I am going out to see my Father's world." Whereupon he would run to the summit of a hill about two miles outside the city and gaze upon the panorama of the combination of Lake Ontario, natural life, and a bird sanctuary where there were forty different varieties of birds. Speaking of the birds, he would say, "I like to hear them raise their carols in praise to God." Upon the return of one of his morning pilgrimages he wrote down his feelings with these lines:

> *This is my Father's world,*
> *And to my listening ears*
> *All nature sings, and round me rings*
> *The music of the spheres.*

THROW OUT THE LIFELINE
Edward Smith Ufford, 1851–1929

In 1886, the Reverend Edward Smith Ufford, Baptist minister, preached a sermon beside the sea in Boston, Massachusetts. At the scene of his sermon was an old ship-wrecked vessel blown in from sea many years before which had become a permanent part of the rock-bound coast. That afternoon as he preached, using the vessel as an object in his sermon, he contemplated the writing of a hymn based on the theme of saving men who had been wrecked at sea. At the time he could not put the lines together, but a little later while visiting a lifesaving station at Nantasket Beach an attendant showed him a slender lifeline and explained its purpose. "This is how we throw out the lifeline," he said as he twirled it about his head. This was just the phrase Ufford had been looking for. Upon returning home he wrote the four stanzas of the hymn in less than fifteen minutes.

'TIS MIDNIGHT AND ON OLIVE'S BROW
William Bingham Tappan, 1794 –1849

This beautiful hymn picturing the suffering and devotion of Jesus in the Garden of Gethsemane was written in 1822 by a Congregational minister, William Bingham Tappan.

The author was born in Beverly, Massachusetts, in 1794, and spent many years of his life associated with the American Sunday School Union. First published in a volume called *Gems of Sacred Poetry,* "Tis Midnight and on Olive's Brow" has long been a favorite of congregations of every denomination, especially during Holy Week.

> *'Tis midnight, and on Olive's brow,*
> *The star is dimmed that lately shone;*
> *'Tis midnight in the garden, now,*
> *The suffering Savior prays alone!*

TRUST AND OBEY
J. H. Sammis, 1850–1919

During a series of meetings conducted by the famous D. L. Moody in Brockton, Massachusetts, a young man rose in the congregation and said, "I am going to trust, and I am going to obey." Present in the group that evening was a professor of music by the name of D. B. Towner. The young man's statement appealed to the professor and he wrote it down and sent it together with the story to a Presbyterian minister, J. H. Sammis. Sammis, recognizing the appeal of the young man's sentence, wrote the well-known chorus which has been a favorite through the years:

> *Trust and obey*
> *For there's no other way*
> *To be happy in Jesus*
> *But to trust and obey.*

WATCHMAN, TELL US OF THE NIGHT
John Bowring, 1792 –1872

This Advent hymn was written by John Bowring in the early nineteenth century. Proficient in five different languages before the age of sixteen, Bowring uses English in this hymn to ask the question first asked in Isaiah 21:11: "Watchman, what of the night?" Before his death, November 23, 1872, Bowring had served as a government official, British consul at Canton, China, and governor at Hong Kong, but he will be remembered far longer for his hymns: "Watchman, Tell Us of the Night" and "In the Cross of Christ I Glory."

WHAT A FRIEND WE HAVE IN JESUS
Joseph Medlicott Scriven, 1819 –1886

Without question this is one of the ten most popular of all the four hundred thousand Christian hymns published in church history. Written in 1855 by Joseph Scriven, Irish by birth but Canadian by adoption, this gospel hymn has been in more constant use by Christian congregations than almost any other imaginable. The hymn was discovered in a very dramatic manner. When Scriven, who lived an extremely tragic life, was in his last days, a friend who was sitting with him during a time of severe illness came upon the manuscript. The friend was very impressed and wondered why it never had been published. Scriven replied, " 'What a Friend we Have in Jesus,' has been written by God and me to comfort my mother during a time of great sorrow." He explained that he never intended that it be used by anyone else. Strange are the ways of fate; a song written only for the life and need of one person became the inspiration of millions! There are conflicting reports about the death of Joseph Scriven. Some authorities say he died of natural causes; others that he took his life in a fit of melancholia. However, they all agree

44

as to the humility and kindness that ruled his days from the great tragedy on the eve of his marriage when his bride-to-be accidently drowned to the day of his death in 1886. The hymn tune usually associated with this song was written in 1868 by Charles G. Converse, born in Warren, Massachusetts. Converse studied in Germany and was acquainted with Franz Liszt.

WHEN I SURVEY THE WONDROUS CROSS
Isaac Watts, 1674 –1748

The noted critic Matthew Arnold said of the two-and-a-half-century-old Christian hymn "When I Survey the Wondrous Cross" that is was "the greatest hymn in the English language." He had such admiration for it that he sang and quoted it on his deathbed. Written in 1707 by Isaac Watts, the hymn was inspired by the words of Paul as recorded in Galatians 6:14, "God forbid that I should glory, save in the cross of our Lord Jesus Christ, by whom the world is crucified unto me, and I unto the world."

WHEN MORNING GILDS THE SKIES
Edward Caswall, 1814 –1878

A famous old German folk song hymn translated into English by Edward Caswall in 1853. One of the first churches to use this hymn was St. Paul's Episcopal Church in London, England, where leaflets were printed and distributed so all the congregation could share in the singing of this beautiful music. One of England's eminent ministers of the nineteenth century, Canon Liddon, considered this one of the greatest of all the church hymns and requested that it be sung at his funeral service.

When morning gilds the skies,
My heart awaking cries,
May Jesus Christ be praised!

WHEN THE ROLL IS CALLED UP YONDER
J. M. Black 1840 –1910 (approximate dates)

J. M. Black wrote the words and music to this gospel hymn in less than fifteen minutes. At a consecration meeting in his church when members were answering the roll call with verses from the Bible, a little fourteen-year-old girl, who had been previously taken in off the streets, failed to respond. The following are the author's own words, "I spoke of what a sad thing it would be, when our names are called from the Lamb's Book of Life, if one of us should be absent." According to Black, he wanted something appropriate to sing just at that time, but could find nothing in the hymnal. The thought came to him, "Why don't you write it yourself?" When he went home that evening, just as he went in the door the words suddenly came to him. Seizing a pen, he wrote them down in a frenzied florish. Going to the piano, he played the music just as it is found in the hymn books today, note for note! Black was so amazed at the speed and ease of his own creation that he dared not change a single word or note from the moment it was written.

WHERE CROSS
THE CROWDED WAYS OF LIFE
Frank Mason North, 1850 –1935

The influence of a hymn on the philosophy of an age cannot be underestimated. It was with this in mind that in 1903, Dr. Frank Mason North wrote the most famous of his hymns "Where Cross the Crowded Ways of Life." He based his hymn on Matthew 22:9:

"Go ye therefore into the highways" and hoped that the singing of this song would express the social content of the gospel.

> *Where cross the crowded ways of life,*
> *Where sound the cries of race and clan,*
> *Above the noise of selfish strife,*
> *We hear thy voice, O son of man!*

The problem of race and strife is still with us in the modern age; and the message of North's stirring hymn is profoundly appropriate.

WHILE SHEPHERDS WATCHED THEIR FLOCKS BY NIGHT
Nahum Tate, 1652 –1715

A beautiful, pictorial Christmas hymn written by Nahum Tate in the late seventeenth century. It first appeared in the Supplement to the New Version of the Psalms in 1700, and was one of six hymns written for Christmas, Easter, and Communion. Only the Christmas hymn, "While Shepherds Watched" based on St. Luke's version of the nativity in Luke 2:8-14, survived. It has become so permanent a part of the celebration of the holy season that it will last as long as Christendom exists.

WORK FOR THE NIGHT IS COMING
Annie Louise Coghill, 1836 –1907

This hymn which emphasizes the joy and the dignity of work and Christian service was written in 1854 by a young girl only eighteen years old. Known then as Annie Louise Walker (later as Annie Louise Coghill) she first published her poem in a Canadian newspaper, and later in her own book called *Leaves from the Back Woods*. Philosophers have made profound statements about the intrinsic value of labor, authors have written paragraphs of prose phrases painting the purpose of labor; poets have sung the praises of the beauty of labor; but none have been able to state more simply and meaningfully the joy of labor in love than has Annie Louise Coghill in her hymn "Work for the Night Is Coming."

AUTHORS

Adam, Adolphe 29
Adams, Sarah F. 26
Alexander, Cecil F. 7, 20, 42
Alford, Henry 11
Babcock, Maltbie D. 43
Baring-Gould, Sabine 27, 31
Bates, Katherine Lee 8
Ben Judah, Daniel 41
Bennett, Sanford F. 39
Bernard of Clairvaux 22, 31
Black, J. M. 45
Bliss, Philip P. 7, 36, 41
Bowring, John 18, 44
Brooks, Phillips 30
Caswall, Edward 45
Clephane, Elizabeth 9, 42
Coghill, Annie Louise 46
Cowper, William 29, 42
Croly, George 38
Crosby, Fanny J. 7, 10 16, 32, 33, 34, 35
Doane, George Washington 37
Doane, William H. 20
Duffield, George R. 38
Dwight, Timothy 17
Ellerton, John 35
Elliott, Charlotte 23
Faber, Frederick W. 12, 43
Fawcett, John 10
Fosdick, Harry Emerson 13
Francis of Assisi 6
Gilmore, Joseph H. 14
Gladden, Washington 30
Gordon, Adoniram J. 26
Grant, Robert 31
Hankey, Katherine 17
Hatch, Edwin 10
Havergal, Frances R. 40
Hawks, Annie S. 17
Heber, Reginald 15
Hopper, Edward 21
Howe, Julia Ward 25
Keble, John 39
Kirkpatrick, William J. 24
Lathbury, Mary A. 10
Longfellow, Henry W. 16
Longfellow, Samuel 15
Longstaff, William D. 40
Lowell, James Russell 31
Lowry, Robert 36
Luther, Martin 5
Lyte, Henry F. 5
Martin, Mrs. C. D. 15

Matheson, George 30
Merrill, William P. 34
Miles, C. Austin 19
Milman, Henry H. 33
Mohr, Joseph 36
Montgomery, James 8, 19
Mote, Edward 26
Neale, John M. 8
Neander, Joachim 32
Newman, John Henry 23
Newton, John 7, 13
North, Frank M. 45
Oxenham, John 18
Palmer, Ray 26
Partridge, Sybil F. 24
Perronet, Edward 6
Phelps, Sylvanus D. 35
Pierpoint, Folliott S. 12
Plumptre, Edward H. 33
Pollard, Adelaide A. 14
Prentiss, Elizabeth P. 25
Rankin, Jeremiah E. 13
Rinkart, Martin 27
Sammis, J. H. 44
Scriven, Joseph M. 44
Sears, Edmund H. 19
Showalter, Anthony J. 24
Shurtleff, Ernest W. 23
Smith, Samuel F. 25, 41
Spafford, Horatio G. 20
Stites, Edgar P. 9
Stone, Samuel J. 40
Stowe, Harriet Beecher 38
Tappan, William B. 43
Tate, Nahum 46
Tennyson, Alfred (Lord) 39
Theodulph of Orleans 6
Thompson, Will L. 37
Thrupp, Dorothy A. 35
Toplady, Augustus M. 34
Ufford, Edward S. 43
Van Dyke, Henry 22
Von Schlegel, Katharina 9
Walford, William W. 40
Walter, Howard A. 18
Warner, Anna 21
Watts, Isaac 6, 11, 21, 22, 29, 45
Wesley, Charles ... 5, 11, 14, 20, 24, 29, 33, 37
Whiting, William 12
Whittier, John Greenleaf 11, 27
Williams, William 13
Wordsworth, Christopher 28